I0653629

About the Author

Muhammed Nozrul Islam was born in Oldham, England. He studied at various Secular and Islamic institutions in the United Kingdom. He graduated from the University of Manchester and then completed a P.G.C.E in Primary Education. He has taught in Primary schools for a number of years and currently holds a post as a Line Operations Manager in a big retail company. His travels to the States, Asia and the Middle East has inspired him to write about events and expeditions that has happened in his life. M N Islam enjoys using his children as the main characters in his stories and hopes to gain an international readership for his children's books.

Acknowledgements

I would like to use this opening to thank Allah, The Lord Almighty for bestowing me with the ability to put my thinking into writing. I take great pleasure in writing about events and episodes in my life through the lens of my children. I thank my parents sincerely, for providing those valuable travelling opportunities in my childhood that have enabled me to put pen to paper in my adulthood. My sincere supplications are reserved for you.

M N Islam, October 2013
www.nextworld.me

Zaynab's Voyage to
St. Martin's Island

By M N Islam

Illustrated by Hasan Ahmed

Published by New Generation Publishing in 2013

Copyright © M. N. Islam 2013

First Edition

The author asserts the moral right under the Copyright,
Designs and Patents Act 1988 to be identified as the
author of this work.

All Rights reserved. No part of this publication may be
reproduced, stored in a retrieval system or transmitted,
in any form or by any means without the prior consent
of the author, nor be otherwise circulated in any form
of binding or cover other than that which it is published
and without a similar condition being imposed on the
subsequent purchaser.

www.newgeneration-publishing.com

 **New Generation Publishing**

Contents

Chapter One

Terminal Two, Dhaka

It was a long haul flight, and Zaynab was now on the second leg of her trip to Bangladesh from Manchester, England. The aeroplane left from Dubai International Airport and had now been flying for nearly four hours. Zaynab was at the start of her adventurous gap year from school.

"This is your captain speaking, we are now descending towards Shahjalal International Airport. Please remain seated after landing, until the aeroplane comes to a complete standstill."

"It looks like we're almost there, Zaynab," said Mum. Zaynab's mum was sitting right next to her. It was a crystal clear view through the window and the lush green vegetation and trees could be seen all around the airport.

"Yes, we're almost there. Mind you everyone, just get prepared for the heat wave that will wallop us when we get off the plane," warned Dad.

It was May, and the heat in Dhaka was extreme and at its peak. There was clear blue sky and dazzling sunshine that beamed down with intense brightness. Zaynab and her family had now landed, and were calmly walking off the aeroplane.

"This is like an oven, my God! I can't even breathe properly," gasped Zaynab.

"Yes, indeed it's hot, its like the scorching heat's pounding on us," shared Dad.

"Get your water bottles out, we don't want anyone collapsing in this heat!" instructed Mum.

Zaynab and her two brothers plodded along with their mum and dad and finally got inside the air-conditioned airport lounge. It was much cooler inside, and more than anything, it was a relief. Zaynab had barely been out in the scorching heat for ten minutes, and she was gushingly sweating and dripping.

"Welcome to Dhaka, Bangladesh," greeted Dad as he sat down, exhausted and weak. "We've still got to collect our luggage and then wait for our local flight to Sylhet," he added.

"This is not an easy trip, is it Zaynab!" exclaimed Zaynab's brother.

"It sure isn't. Bayyah! The trip seems to be going on forever, and it doesn't help when it's this hot and sticky either!"

"Don't worry children, it'll be worth all the trouble, once we arrive in Sylhet. You'll soon forget the hard and tiresome experience," reassured Mum.

"Why, what's in Sylhet that's gonna be different from here, Mum?" enquired Zaynab.

"In Sylhet, you won't be carrying dozens of bags and waiting around for hours in one place. You'll be free to begin your holiday fun, as we'll be stopping for a week in a luxury apartment. There's a swimming pool, lots of children's activities, and of course, lots of shops. You'll be having plenty of fun, I assure you," explained Mum.

"Yeah, that sure sounds good, how long before we get there Dad?" Zaynab asked.

"We do have to wait a few more hours for our flight to Sylhet, but once we're on the aeroplane, it only takes about forty-five minutes."

"Oh, I guess, that's not too bad, as long as there's no delays," muttered Zaynab, very happy to wait a few more hours.

Zaynab pulled out a hand fan and began to cool herself down further. Everyone just looked exhausted, not because they had walked or ran a lot, but because of the dreadful heat. The airport lounge was certainly much cooler than outside, but it was still humid and very uncomfortable. It felt sticky and everyone was breathless.

"Let's go and buy some ice cold drinks and lollipops, Dad," suggested Zaynab.

"That sounds like a good idea to me. Anyone want anything in particular?" asked Dad.

"Yeah, I'll have a cold lemonade," shouted Mum.

"And I'll have a cola lollipop," bellowed Zaynab's brother.

"I'll have some pineapple juice with ice," mumbled Luqman, the youngest in the family.

"Not sure about your cola flavours and your pineapple juices, but we'll give it a try anyway," answered Dad and made his way to the shops with Zaynab.

The airport felt rather empty and almost deserted. There weren't many people crowding round the desks and luggage conveyers like other busier airports. This was because most of the people had left for Sylhet by coach or their last stop had been Dhaka. Zaynab and her family had chosen to fly to Sylhet because Zaynab's dad had said the hundred and twenty-five mile road trip to Sylhet wasn't that great due to the potholed and bumpy roads.

"There's not a lot of shops inside this airport Dad?" muttered Zaynab. She could practically count them all on her fingers.

"They've just got the essential ones here, Zaynab, that's all."

"Look over there Dad, it looks like it's an ice cream stand, can we go there?" shrieked Zaynab with excitement.

Once they arrived at the ice cream stand, Zaynab was rather disappointed to learn that there was no more ice cream or any lollipops left.

"Let's just take some cold drinks for everyone and save the ice cream party for later hey," suggested Dad.

"Well, we don't have much choice I guess," mumbled Zaynab rather reluctantly.

"That will be, five hundred takas, Sir," demanded the shopkeeper.

"That's a bit pricey for five drink bottles, isn't it?" Zaynab's dad quizzed.

"Well, it's priced at a hundred takas per bottle, Sir, and that's because they are chilled in the fridge," explained the shopkeeper.

"Very well then, here's a five hundred taka note, please give me a carrier bag."

"Five hundred takas! That sounds like a lot of money!" shrieked Zaynab. "How much is that in pounds, Dad?"

"It's around five pounds, Zaynab," replied Dad.

"I thought things were really cheap here in Bangladesh, Dad? This seems like the same cost as we would pay in our local shop back home," grumbled Zaynab.

"You're right but it is an airport after all, so as long as we don't drink too much, I think we'll be fine," said

Dad prudently.

A few hours had passed and there were no announcements made. Everyone began to get a little agitated. The flight to Sylhet seemed to be delaying a little by the hour.

"Shall we go and find out exactly what time the plane's supposed to arrive Dad?" suggested Zaynab.

"Yeah I think we shall, we've patiently waited long enough. Come on let's go."

A few moments later, Zaynab's dad reached the ticket office for Emirates Airlines and learnt that the flight had been further delayed due to an electrical fault on the aeroplane.

"How long is the delay likely to be then?" asked Dad.

"Sir, the delay could be up to five hours," informed the airline officer in his distinctive Bangladeshi accent.

"Five hours! This can't be happening!" exclaimed Zaynab's dad rather frustrated and annoyed.

"Right, we're going to have to make a speedy decision. Zaynab, let's go back to the waiting area and decide what to do," he declared and marched back to join the rest of the family.

"I think we should contact the Emirates' Coach Office and book ourselves in to go by road," suggested Dad.

"But it's going to be a really long and bumpy ride you said, remember," reminded Zaynab.

"Yeah, I think we should go for the bumpy ride, at least we'll be out of this airport immediately," insisted Mum.

"How long is the so called bumpy ride to Sylhet then, Dad?" asked Zaynab's brother.

"It's about five and a half hours trip by coach,"

replied Dad.

"Well, that means we can still get to Sylhet before the aeroplane would get us there, and that's providing it comes in the next five hours," retorted Zaynab.

"Yes, I think we're all eager to get out of this humid, boring and gloomy airport. Everyone follow me," ordered Zaynab's dad, and the family marched forth, exiting the airport.

The Emirates bus was not bad at all; it was spacious and very luxurious. More importantly, it was air-conditioned and it blew a nice consistent current of cold air on full power. The cold chilly breeze felt ever so good and refreshing after staying in that stodgy airport lounge for so many hours.

"I think this feels better than the aeroplane, why didn't we think of this sooner?" called out Zaynab.

"Actually, you're right, we can admire the countryside and see all the spectacular scenery throughout the whole trip. We can even stop for breaks and refreshments," said Dad.

"I think it was a good idea that we've chosen the road trip. I mean, the children can see so much more of the green land," asserted Mum.

"I guess so, this trip is about observing and discovering after all. Sit back everyone and enjoy the ride," announced Dad.

The trip to Sylhet from Dhaka was just under a hundred and twenty five miles. This would have normally been a smooth and easy ride but the roads were not in the best of shape. They were riddled with potholes and packed with traffic of all sorts. Huge trucks impudently horned as they passed by, and it felt as though they dominated the roads. It was rather different from being on a British road, thought Zaynab. She certainly wouldn't be seeing the bull carts, horses and cattle as frequently as she did on the roads in Bangladesh.

Zaynab's dad had booked their first week's stay in Sylhet and then they would head to the village for their long, adventurous vacation.

"It's a shame we can't spend a few days in Dhaka to explore the city. This city is full of history and delights," Zaynab's dad revealed. "Sonargaon, the golden village, has history dating back to the 13th century when the Mughals ruled. The Zoological Garden in Mir Pur, would have been interesting. Or even, a tour to Bait ul Mukarram, the National Mosque of Bangladesh, would have been literally rewarding to visit."

"Maybe, we should come back after a few weeks and explore Dhaka properly. I like learning about capital cities and Dhaka is obviously the capital city," suggested Zaynab.

"Yes, maybe we should. There's a lot more great places, for instance, Bahadur Shah Park, The National Museum, Fantasy Kingdom, The Heritage Park, The Nandon Park, Botanical Garden and then there's the National Art Gallery. The list is endless. With all this fun and adventure, I think a re-visit to Dhaka will certainly be on the cards. I guess you'll welcome that, Zaynab?"

"Maybe we should all camp out in Dhaka instead of going anywhere else," suggested Mum with a hint of sarcasm. Zaynab's brother felt left out of the conversation so he mustered in.

"Erm... Why isn't my opinion being sought? I like the sound of some of the places you've talked about and I fancy the National Art Gallery!"

"Actually, it does sound really educational, and with so much to see, maybe we should come back in a few weeks or even a few month's time," insisted Mum, this time without the sarcasm.

"Maybe, we will," added Dad.

"Hurray!" cheered Zaynab and her brothers, as they continued to enjoy the natural green beauty though the coach window. One particular destination that stuck in Zaynab's mind was the Fantasy Kingdom. It was just something about that place. It sounded magical and mysterious. Zaynab was keen to visit the Fantasy Kingdom at some point, there was something intriguing and exciting about it. She made a careful note of the name in her diary and filed it away for a later date.

Dhaka certainly sounded fun and interesting. There was so much to see and so much to learn. But that was not possible just yet. That's because, Zaynab and her family were now minutes away from Sylhet where they were going to spend the first week before they headed to the village. The village would be an ideal escape from the urban chaotic life, thought Zaynab's dad, and he looked forward keenly to all the exotic seasons, weather, water and luscious fruits. It would provide a firm base for a gap year exploration and to marvel at the wonders of rural living.

Chapter Two

Tea Garden, Sylhet

The arrival into Sylhet wasn't as bad as everyone had thought. The ride was sure bumpy, but the gigantic coach had taken much of the beating instead of the passengers. The scenery along the way was fascinating with rivers, huge wetlands called *haors,* fisheries, rice mills, mud and straw houses forming part of the natural view. To Zaynab it felt as though what she had been reading in books had really come to life.

Sylhet looked absolutely stunning with its tropical forests and famous tea gardens. The British had passed on the tea plantations from the 19th century. They were a great heritage as it made Sylhet prosper immensely, but more importantly it gave rise to the beautiful, lush green landscape, which, was breathtaking and picturesque.

"Children! Look over there! You can see the tea-pluckers," shouted Dad.

"Yeah, they look so gorgeous and colourful, it looks like they're all women," muttered Zaynab.

"Yes, the women mainly pluck the tea leaves, while the men do the more tougher jobs like farming and construction work here," explained Mum.

"Wow, Mum! Look at the different colour *sarees* they're wearing, it looks stunning against all the greenness they're surrounded in," observed Zaynab.

"Bless them, they work ever so hard and for terribly long hours too," said Mum.

"But I'm sure they get free tea everyday!" muttered Zaynab's brother.

"You'd be surprised, son, some of these poor workers have never tasted the tea they've been plucking for years," explained Dad. "They are for commercial use and workers can't really take these home. Besides, they need to go through a mechanical process to turn the leaves into the tea that we drink."

"Oh, well, hope they get some good money for doing this job then."

"Not really, they probably earn around a hundred takas per day, that's like a pound each day. So life is tough for them here," explained Dad.

"We need to appreciate their hard work and thank Allah that we're not going through the painstaking work they're going through," urged Dad. And so the family spent a few moments contemplating and thanking Allah by offering a silent prayer.

The coach had arrived at Uposhohor Road. The trip from Dhaka was now complete. In front of them was the tall and glamorous Garden Tower building, which offered many facilities for children and adults. Zaynab remembered her mum saying something about a swimming pool and a children's games room.

"Wow, it certainly looks like a posh place this; look

Zaynab, look at all the turquoise glass from top to bottom of this building, just looks incredible," called out Zaynab's brother.

"Yeah, looks very nice, but more than that, I can't wait to jump in that pool. I wonder how big and deep it is?" asked Zaynab.

"Not really sure about the size, we'll just have to find out everyone," stated Dad.

Moments later, the whole family checked in to their spacious apartment, pulled in their luggage and began to rest for a while.

"There's no time to waste! I don't know about you lot, but I'm heading right for the pool," declared Dad.

"I want to go," yelled Zaynab's brother.

"I want to go too," yelled Zaynab. And so, both of them hopped along with their dad to the Garden Tower swimming pool. It looked like Zaynab's mum had other plans and wasn't interested in going back out in a hurry. She was too busy thinking about how to organise the rooms so it looked welcoming and neat. The rooms just looked too messy. There were clothes; bags and luggage simply dropped all over in the frantic rush. She got busy unpacking properly while Zaynab's younger brother played quietly with his lego.

Garden Tower apartments had all the facilities that anyone could ask for. There were all types of shops on the ground floor - there was a sports shop, swimming baths, and a large hall, which had all the table games like pool, ping pong, carom board and ice hockey. It instantly felt cosy and welcoming and the family had no trouble whatsoever adjusting to the life in the urban and lively town of Sylhet. The apartment itself was situated on a busy road, which simply meant easy access to the main shopping malls and restaurants. It was the perfect place for a family from England. It was a bustling metropolitan city with lots to see and discover.

"Can we go out to some shops now?" asked Zaynab.

"Yeah, we haven't eaten anything for ages, I want to go to a restaurant," bellowed her brother.

"Well of course we're gonna eat and we'll visit shops too, but all in good time, children," reassured Dad.

It wasn't long before two rickshaws parked up right in front of the tower, ready to take Zaynab's family to the big shopping malls. Rickshaws were like giant tricycles and were very easy to come by near the busy road. They were easier to use for accessing the inner market alleys. Zaynab's dad thought it would be nice to bond with the *Sylheti* culture and where possible utilised rickshaws and CNGs. CNGs were a mix between a rickshaw and a British milk float. It had three wheels and some people simply called it the auto rickshaw. It seemed like there were more CNGs on the road than any other vehicle.

"Why do all those green cars have weird names on them?" asked Zaynab.

"Those green cars are called CNGs or you could call them auto rickshaws if you want. And what do you mean by weird names on them?" questioned Dad.

"Well, I've seen one that says, 'fortune city' another that said 'mother's love' and look over there now, there's one going past, it says:'Tajmahal'. I mean these sound so random, what's that all about?" Zaynab asked curiously.

"My word, girl! You do pick out some tedious things, people just write on them phrases that are important to them, that's all," explained Dad.

"Well maybe the person who's named the 'fortune city' CNG, wishes one day they become rich and have a fortune!" joked Zaynab.

"Well, maybe, that was the reason behind it. But I agree, it does sound a little weird!" added Dad with a smug smile.

"There's about sixteen big shopping centres in Sylhet, which one shall we go to?" announced Dad scrolling through a miniature map of the shopping malls.

"Go on, read some of them out, and the one that sounds nicest, we'll go to that," shouted everyone.

"Erm...there's Al-Hambra Shopping City, Sylhet Plaza, Blue Water Shopping City, Sylhet Millennium Mall, Shukria Market...What do you think?" asked Dad.

"Go on Dad, read out a few more then?"

"Well, there's also the Karim Ullah Market, Garden Tower Shopping Mall, One City, and there's also the Manru Shopping City," he further added.

"Well, I like Blue Water Shopping City," called out Zaynab's brother.

"I like the sound of Al-Hambra Shopping City," said Zaynab.

"I think Sylhet Millennium Mall sounds better, let's go there," insisted Mum.

"Never mind asking you lot, I knew the choices wouldn't match. Let's just go to all three, hey!" decided Dad and off they headed towards the busy shopping complex.

The short trip to the malls provided a chance to see Sylhet in its full glory. The endless rows of shops, cafes, restaurants and fast food outlets were all bustling with people. There were congested roads and people haggling in every store. The rickshaws travelled at a brisk pace and the cool breeze was soothing in the sweltering heat.

"I think we'll stop here," shouted Zaynab's dad and gestured to the second rickshaw to do the same.

They were now right opposite the Blue Water

Shopping City.

"This is amazing! I love that long red LED display," cried out Zaynab. "It's got a message on, erm... *'World class shopping experience'*" she read out, not able to keep up with the speed at which the message was passing on the display.

"Yeah that's a cool gadget, hey wait! It says, *'capsule lift core',* what on earth is that?" called out Zaynab's brother.

"That means the lift inside this building's in a capsule shape with steel and glass," explained Dad.

"Wow, they do use a lot of glass in this country, everything seems to be in a green or blue shaded glass, I'm sure it'll look fabulous," said Zaynab's brother.

"Yes, I'm sure it will. Do you know that I can read *'food court'* on that display? I think we should begin by having our lunch and then start shopping!" suggested Mum.

"Great idea," shouted everyone.

The inside of the Shopping Mall was breathtaking. It was gigantic and very well presented. It was so modern that Zaynab forgot that she was in Bangladesh. All the shop displays were in English as well as Bangla. The air-conditioning worked perfectly and the humidity completely vanished. The powerful dazzling lights were so bright that it was hard to tell if it was sunlight or just the powerful gleam of the light bulbs. There were shops of every kind, and Zaynab was already eyeing a few that she particularly took an interest in.

"I'm hungry," cried out the little one.

"Yeah, me too. I think we should look for a restaurant in here first," said Zaynab.

"Yes, let's move on till we get to the food court," instructed Dad.

It wasn't long before they came across a nice posh looking restaurant. And the family quickly sat down to eat. The menu was brought over to their table and everyone fell in deep thought trying to work out what to have.

"Try some of the traditional Bengali food everyone, let's leave the pizzas, burgers and the other fast foods out, hey!" suggested Dad.

"We don't fancy those types of food anyway," shouted everyone. Zaynab's dad flicked through the menu and it didn't take too long to make a choice.

"I'll have the king prawn curry with rice, I'm sure the freshly cooked spices will make it outstandingly delicious," hoped Dad.

"We'll have the beef desi biryani," called out Zaynab and her brother.

"I'm having the *boal* fish curry with rice," said Mum. I like the big *boal* fish and I'm hoping as you point out, the spices here should be fresh and tastier."

And so the family huddled up together around the table and enjoyed a beautiful meal cooked in traditional fresh Bengali spices. They thoroughly enjoyed the experience and could not ask for a better restaurant to dine in. After the meal, the shopping spree began and everyone was spoilt for choice once again.

"Now that's what you call a selection of crockery and tableware," yelped Mum. "There's such a huge variety of glassware and ceramics, this should be fun looking through," she muttered.

"Yeah, look at those beautiful plates, I like the flowery design on those," joined in Zaynab.

This bored Zaynab's brother and her dad and they decided to walk on to different shops.

"Dad! Look at that remote control helicopter, can I

have one?" eagerly asked Zaynab's brother.

"I suppose you could, but you do know that they're ever so delicate, if you crash it in to anything, it'll be history!" explained Dad.

"I'll be really careful with it Dad, please!"

"Go on then, let's get two, so we can both fly it outside and compare them, when we get back to the apartment. But I'll pass mine on to Luqman after I've had a go," confirmed Dad.

It was hard to tell whether Dad really wanted to play himself with the excuse of buying it for Luqman. After all, Luqman was too young to fly a remote controlled helicopter.

Hours had passed, and Zaynab and her family were fully quenched from the thirst of shopping. They had so many bags to carry back that rickshaws would no longer be suitable. So Zaynab's dad thought the ideal thing to do was to hire two CNGs, giving everyone the feel of the auto rickshaws.

On the way back, Zaynab's dad suggested they stop at his favourite cafe for a quick cup of desi tea. New Green Cafe in the *Taltola* area was where Zaynab's dad used to come with Zaynab's granddad whenever they visited Sylhet.

"This tea is undoubtedly the best tea I've ever had," shrieked Dad with excitement. There was something about the tea in New Green Cafe. It was more than just the fresh tealeaves coming straight from the Sylhet tea gardens; it was more nostalgic than anything else. Zaynab's dad remembered his childhood holidays and how he used to come to the New Green Cafe with his father.

"Erm...can we go now Dad?" voiced the children with a sullen tone. "It's not exactly enjoyable for us watching you sip tea in this over crowded place, and they've got fans on that are blowing hot wind!"

Not every cafe in Sylhet looked modern or glamorous, some were just making ends meet and were not in the best of shape. The fine dining experiences were mainly inside the big shopping malls and the smaller cafes outside were pretty much unchanged in their appearance, no matter how many generations had passed by. This helped put everything into perspective, and the reality soon hit home as the children realised where they were.

"You shouldn't judge a cafe and its quality of food and drink, because it lacks a modern look in its appearance. These are very nice people and they make very nice tea," explained Dad.

"Waiter," he called out. "Can you fill this flask with some more tea," he instructed. The rest of the family could only smirk at the sight. Zaynab's dad was no doubt a tea fan.

"Sylhet is the city for tea, and I'm only too proud to have the freshly brewed tea leaves coming from its very own tea gardens. Long live the Sylhet tea gardens!" hailed Zaynab's dad.

Chapter Three

A village called Budharail

A week had very quickly passed by, and Zaynab's family had enjoyed much more of Sylhet life than they could have ever imagined. They had shopped in various malls, eaten in both luxurious and modest restaurants and made the most out of the Garden Tower club. It was so far the perfect holiday with plenty of sun, water and fun. In fact, there was just a bit too much sun for everyone's liking.

"I can't believe we've been in the Garden Towers for a week! My Lord, time has flown past," said Dad.

"I wish we could stay here for longer, I was just beginning to enjoy myself. It's so fun here," said Zaynab.

"Unfortunately dear, we have only booked here for a week, we will be travelling to the village today, and staying there for the rest of our time in this country," confirmed Dad. "You'll really enjoy the village life, away from the noise and bustling atmosphere of the city," he explained.

"Yes, your dad's made a special arrangement with your school to have you out for a full year. It's only right that we stay in the village to explore the natural rural settings for the best part of the trip," explained Mum.

"But why exactly in the village?" Zaynab asked again.

"Besides the benefit a rural outdoor experience, the house in the village belongs to your granddad, and we can stay for free as long as we like. If we stay anywhere else we have to pay!" Dad explained.

"Right, I understand, we can't pay and stay somewhere for a year, too expensive!" called out Zaynab.

"Anyway, there's so much planned for the stay in the village. Your dad will be expecting some daily school work from you both, besides the fun and adventure," revealed Mum.

"No way! Schoolwork! Did I hear school work?" screeched Zaynab's brother.

"Yes, school work means you'll be doing a little Literacy, Numeracy and Science with me every day. I didn't want to spoil it for you in the first week, but now that we've had a wonderful and relaxing past week we can look forward to the village life and your schooling too," confirmed Dad.

"Don't worry children, it won't feel like you're doing school work anyway, your dad will be reasonable with you, I'm sure," reassured Mum. "And with the village life there's no doubt your science lessons are going to be interesting, hey?"

"Yes, I wouldn't worry too much, children, we'll be doing lots of outdoor work and experiments. You might even end up liking my school more than your school back in England," said Dad almost chuckling.

"I guess we'll just have to find out when we get there," remarked Zaynab and her brother.

Budharail was the village where Zaynab's grandfather grew up. It was like a subtropical island with many types of fruit and vegetation. The whole village was surrounded by tall betel nut trees, palm and coconut trees. The crispy lush green leaves of the Amra tree were more visible than any other trees. There were lychee and mango trees, the single stem papaya tree and an abundance of watermelon trees. The most popular ones were the jackfruit trees, the jackfruit being the national fruit of Bangladesh.

Zaynab's family had travelled from Sylhet for just under a couple of hours, and they had now reached the lush green, effervescent village of Budharail.

"I can't believe my eyes! You never said the village was this nice, Dad?" cried out Zaynab.

"It's breathtaking, so many dazzling colours of flowers, vegetables and the different types of fruit trees, wow I'm sure we're gonna have lots of fun here, I can see it."

"I love it, the brightness, the colours, the openness, the air, the liveliness about it, it's just so welcoming and nice. I can see myself exploring this place, Dad," muttered Zaynab's brother.

"I'm glad your first impressions of the village are positive, but let me tell you that this is only the start. You can obviously see the rivers, ponds and fisheries too right? Well think of the fun we can have fishing, swimming and boat riding."

"We thought you'd be excited children. You don't get this sort of experience in many places, especially for such a long time as we've planned for! So I say to you, make the most out of it," urged Mum.

As the family neared their tall four-storey house, a flurry of people ran forward and began to greet, hug and kiss the family.

"Yuck!" cried out Zaynab's brother

"Eew!"Jeered Zaynab. "Who on earth are these people, why are they hugging Mum and Dad and why are they hugging us?" Zaynab enquired.

"Don't be so rude, children, they are your relatives, most of them are your aunties and uncles, you'll get to know them pretty soon," Explained Mum.

"Well that's a first, I didn't know we had that many aunties and uncles! Never mind," muttered Zaynab as she wiped off her cheek due to the little peck from one of the aunties. It was a little bit like a royal reception, so many curious people from the village gathered just to see who had arrived. It wasn't often they saw visitors from England and this time they weren't about to miss anything. All the people cheered and waved at Zaynab's family, some shouting out greetings and conveying the traditional Islamic salaam. At the very beginning it overwhelmed Zaynab, but she soon understood that these were friendly local village people who would in fact be her neighbours for the next exciting year.

Zaynab and her family were going to stay in a huge four-storey house. It was lavishly designed and the house looked spectacular all round. It was very modern and had an appearance like a villa home in somewhere like Spain. It also had the beautiful blue shaded glass for many of its windows that Zaynab so much liked back in the Sylhet, Blue Water Shopping Centre.

"This house is huge and my voice is echoing inside," cried out Zaynab in sheer excitement.

"Yeah just look at the room sizes, my God, they are big!" exclaimed her brother.

"Let's explore the house," suggested Zaynab. "Let's see what's upstairs on the other floors?"

"Come on, this way, follow me," commanded Zaynab's brother as though he already knew what was where. Both brother and sister did not waste any time. They had hardly put their bags down and were already embroiled in the exploration of the gigantic house. Both of them got to the top floor of the house. There was another set of stairs that led to the roof from there. Curiously, both tiptoed their way up the steps and out on the roof.

"Wow! This is awesome. This sight is spectacular, we're so high up and I can see the whole village from here," shouted Zaynab. Looking down from the flat rooftop was exhilarating. All the landscape, the tall green trees, the river and fields could be seen at a glance. Zaynab had a pair of binoculars around her neck and further magnified her view.

"Yeah, I can hear the birds singing, and the mild winds gently rattling the treetops, this is amazing Zaynab, this is just fascinating," praised Zaynab's brother.

Just then, someone from a distance was calling.

"Erm...your mummy en daddy are calling you," said the voice. Zaynab and her brother looked back, they had not met this little boy standing at the bottom of the stairway before. He appeared to be a little shy.

"Hey, what's your name?" Zaynab asked.

"My nam ij Dulon, I find hard ispeaking Engreji, but I istill try," he replied. Dulon was a village neighbour who was in primary school, and only spoke a few sentences in English. His language was Bangla, but he made an effort to speak to Zaynab in English.

"Hey Dulon, you seem to have understood Zaynab well, and your speaking isn't too bad either," claimed Zaynab's brother.

"Yes, I try bery hard, I am loving Enreji language," said Dulon.

"Well, let's put it this way, you speak better English than I do Bangla. Maybe we can teach each other over the coming months," suggested Zaynab's brother.

"Yes, bery good, I like to ispeak like you," Dulon said very cheerfully.

The three of them headed downstairs. It was late in the afternoon and the rays of the sun shone with less might. Zaynab's dad suggested they go out for a stroll to the fruit garden to admire more of the pleasant scenery, pick some exotic fruits and wind down near the palm trees. It was Zaynab's grandfather's fruit garden and back in England she had been told to eat as much fruit as she could by her granddad. There were so many types of fruit trees; some Zaynab hadn't even come across before. Dulon was asked to join them in the fruit garden and plodded along all excited to spend time with his new friends. Zaynab's family sat down, admiring the great work that had gone into the garden. There was even a bungalow there that had all the basic facilities like a ceiling fan, bathroom and a dining table. Zaynab entered the bungalow alongside her dad and brother and sat down around the table.

"This room is nice and cool and it feels so cosy here," called out Zaynab.

"Yeah, I'm so tired and exhausted I'm gonna lie down on that bed," said Zaynab's brother

"Dulon, could you please switch the fan on?" asked Dad.

Dulon was only too happy to run around and do the odd chores; it was his chance to be together with Zaynab and her brother.

"Shall I get some narkelle?" he asked politely.

"What's a narkelle?" asked Zaynab.

"It's a coconut, darling, it's called narkelle in Bangla," explained Dad.

"Yes, Dulon. Please do, we can all enjoy the coconut water which will nicely hydrate us," said Dad.

"Coconut water is really good for you, it's even better than having a sports drink. It'll keep your body cool and maintain a good temperature. It's got high levels of potassium," explained Dad.

"I think our science lesson has already started, Bayyah," signalled Zaynab.

"Hey Zaynab, you call your brathar 'bayyah', that's nice, becoz in our calture, its good to ispeak lovingly like that," said Dulon.

"Yeah, Dulon I've always called him Bayyah because I know it's more appreciated than calling him by his name because he's older than me," explained Zaynab.

"That's right, Zaynab, as Dulon points out, it's a cultural thing to use the word 'bayyah' for addressing your brother. It shows respect. This is encouraged a lot in the Bengali culture," added Dad.

And so the banter continued while everyone enjoyed sipping the delicious, sweet and tasty coconut water, which was freshly poured straight out of the coconuts. There was certainly no shortage of coconuts; there were hundreds in the giant fruit garden.

"Since we're on the topic of coconuts, let me tell you some more fascinating facts about this marvellous fruit," insisted Dad. "The whole coconut tree is a very valuable element of life here, nearly every part of it is used for something. The leaves are often used for making thatched roofs, the trunk is used for fires and cooking fuel, and the fibres are even used to make fishing nets," he explained. "And of course, the actual white coconut meat is used for food and oil too!"

"Wow, I could have never thought of that, all those uses just from one fruit!" bellowed Zaynab, quite astounded at the fascinating facts.

Suddenly there was a moment of silence. "Can you all hear that?" pointed out Dad.

31

"Hear what?" yelped Zaynab's brother.

"Listen carefully, can you hear frogs croaking and the crickets chirping? Sounds like we're right in the middle of an amazon forest!"

"Yeah, I can hear them," whispered Zaynab. "Sounds so busy and quirky."

It was a fine taste of village life to be surrounded by croaking frogs and chirping crickets, and all the other tiny creatures that were going about their normal habitats. It was a moment to enjoy in the shade of the palm trees, drinking cool coconut water and admiring the picturesque scenery. Budharail wasn't a bad village, the children thought, after all. It was a place for discovery, fascination and real life experience.

"We love it here, Dad," voiced Zaynab and her brother, totally thrilled with their first day in the village.

Chapter four

The Big Wedding

The rural life in many ways began to grow on Zaynab and her family, and every territory of the village became familiar and adaptable. Friends and family were constantly in and out of the gigantic house, and the village life seemed to be bustling with wonders and mysteries. On one evening, as the sun began to set and the call to prayer echoed across the open plains, there was a knock on the four storey mansion door. It was a tall man, dressed rather smartly, and carrying a briefcase.

"I wonder who that is, knocking at the time of prayer!" muttered Mum.

"Dad's gone to the mosque to pray, Mum, we're not really expecting anyone at this time, shall we answer it?" asked Zaynab's brother. The rule at home was not to open the doors to strangers after dark. And since Zaynab's dad was not at home, there was altogether more reason to ignore the knock on the door.

"Psst, Zaynab!" whispered Mum. "Have a peep

through the window and check who's there!" she ordered.

"Okay, Mum," answered Zaynab softly, and leaned over to peep through the window.

"Mum, it's a tall man with a briefcase in his hand," whispered back Zaynab.

"Who on earth is that? Children do not open the door, it's a stranger!" gasped Mum.

For the next few minutes, they waited patiently for the man to go away or for Zaynab's dad to come back from the mosque or whichever was sooner. Meanwhile Zaynab's dad got chatting to the mosque Imam after the prayer and was taking longer to return home than he usually did.

"Knock, knock!" came the thudding sound once more.

"Just keep quiet everyone and he'll soon go away," whispered Mum.

"Where's Dad? How come he's not back yet?" cried out Zaynab.

The stranger had now understood, no one was going to open the door to him, so he stopped knocking and waited quietly outside in the veranda. Just then, some footsteps could be heard in the distance. The children instantly knew that Dad was coming home.

"Thank God, Dad's here, we need to find out who this stranger is," said Zaynab.

"Assalamu alaikum!" greeted Zaynab's dad to the stranger.

"Wa alaikumus salaam!" replied the stranger.

"Hey, Ashraf! That's a nice surprise! What brings you here? And when did you come from England?" asked Zaynab's dad.

"Oh, don't talk about it, I just arrived yesterday with

my family. My sister's getting married next week. I didn't think I was gonna attend all the way out here, but I managed to get the time off work, so I just booked and here I am," Ashraf explained.

"Where are you staying, Ashraf?"

"Well, we booked in at the Garden Tower apartments in Sylhet, but the wedding's gonna be in the village next week."

"Hey, we just had a week's stay at the same place. I guess it's a good stop over for everyone before they come to the village. Which village are you coming to then?" asked Dad.

"It's Sayedpur, just round the corner from your village," confirmed Ashraf.

"Yes, of course it is... Let's go in my friend," urged Dad.

There was a sigh of relief inside the home while the banter continued. Zaynab took a deep breath and relaxed, it was her dad's friend from England who had come to invite her family to the wedding.

"You must all attend next Sunday, it'll be a grand wedding with lots of fireworks and entertainment," requested Ashraf. "You children will love the experience and not to forget, you'll meet some of my nephews and nieces who are here from London too."

"That sounds brilliant, Ashraf. We're fully settled into the village life now and we needed an event like this to spice up a bit of the country life. I happily accept your invitation and you shall see us all there on Sunday," confirmed Dad.

"Hurray!" cried out the children. "This is going to be fun, our first ever wedding in Bangladesh!"

Zaynab's mum had just finished making tea and brought it forward together with some delicious coconut biscuits.

"You terrified us," confessed Mum. "I've never met

you in England, so I didn't know who you were!"

"Not to worry, I should have come in the day time, sorry my fault. It's just that by the time I arranged a car to get to the village, it was already evening," explained Ashraf.

"Oh it's not your fault, it takes time to arrange trips in this place," said Dad. "You're staying with us for the night, right?"

"Oh definitely not, I have booked a driver to pick me up from Sayedpur. I'll be stopping by there, meeting everyone before I head back first thing in the morning," explained Ashraf.

"Well that's not too bad then, Sayedpur is only ten minutes away from here," said Dad.

A few days had passed by, and Zaynab and her brother got stuck into their schoolwork. Literacy and Numeracy were pretty boring for them, they had to complete set work from the textbooks and then read books and do mental arithmetic. The most popular lesson by far was science. Zaynab's dad set them up with plenty of outdoor investigations and experiments. Just as well, one of the term topics on science was 'habitats'. The children thoroughly enjoyed going to the ponds and fishing for tadpoles and frogs. They got to see how the ants marched from tree to land and how they carried beautiful green leaves back to their colonies to produce a type of fungus that they lived on.

"It's strange, Bayyah! The ants seem to carry leaves all the time yet they don't seem to eat them?" Zaynab asked.

"Yeah that's true, they actually carry them back to their base, the leaves help them to make their food," explained Zaynab's brother.

"What is their food, if it's not leaves then?" asked Zaynab, rather puzzled.

"I can't quite remember, but I think they make some sort of fungus out of it, and that's the stuff they eat," he explained. "They're fascinating insects, I mean they can carry up to fifty times their body weight. There's not many things that can do that."

"Yeah, I just love watching them march about, no wonder some of the types are called Army Ants," said Zaynab with a grin on her face. Nothing could beat the outdoor experience Zaynab and her brother enjoyed. They were learning new things each day and were enjoying the process thoroughly.

Sunday finally arrived, and the family woke up early to get ready for the big wedding day over in Sayedpur. There was a family outdoor pool facing the fruit garden and Zaynab's dad announced that he would be going for a swim there. As usual, Zaynab and her brother trudged along with their dad to enjoy a session of swimming.

"The water's nice and warm Dad," shouted Zaynab.

"Yes, it's not bad for this time, it's usually a bit chilly in the mornings," explained Dad. "Stay near the stairs, you don't want to drift off too far. It is a giant pool."

Zaynab and her brother enjoyed splashing about. They clung on to a banana log, which was floating about in the pool. Banana trees were cut and used for floats to train children to swim, and they were also used for playing in the water.

"Hey this is cool, I bet if I could get a few of these together I could make a nice raft," suggested Zaynab's brother.

"That'll be fun, I'll tell someone to fetch you some more banana logs for next time," said Dad.

"As much as we would like to spend all day in this pool, we have a job to do children!" reminded Dad. "We need to head back to the house and jump in the showers quickly. I'm guessing your mum and Luqman are probably dressed, ready and waiting for us by now."

And so the three of them rushed back home, dripping in pool water, and speedily ran into three different bathrooms to shower. A few moments later the whole family was ready and waiting for their car for Sayedpur to arrive.

The journey to Sayedpur was most enjoyable. Passing through the village and observing all the wonderful scenery was breathtaking. The beautifully painted houses in many bright colours added to the splendour of the rural homes. Zaynab's family passed by small convenience stores and huts, cafes and goldsmiths, bookshops and barbers, banks and clinics. There were all the different types of shops and facilities that you could find in the city. The villages are catching up with the town and cities, they all thought. A few moments later, the car stopped in front of a three storey extravagantly decorated building. It was not even recognisable due to the amount of wedding decoration that was covering it.

"That's got to be the house, it's obvious with all the decorations," gestured Zaynab's dad.

"It sure does look like it, Dad, it's so colourful, I think it has more colours on it than the rainbow," remarked Zaynab.

Just then, Ashraf appeared from nowhere. "Yes, it probably has more colours to it than the rainbow," he acknowledged. Zaynab felt a little embarrassed because her description was rather exaggerated and more so, because uncle Ashraf had heard her.

"Come out everyone and just follow me," instructed Ashraf.

Zaynab and her family walked inside and noticed that the house was full with guests. There were children running from room to room, women chatting in clusters, men huddled up together drinking tea and having *Huqqah* pipe. The smell of strongly flavoured tobacco engulfed the entire main lounge where the family stood.

"Children, you can go to the room opposite, it's the kids chilling out area, you can talk and get to know other children like yourselves. Besides, this room isn't suitable for you," explained Ashraf.

"Good idea, go on, off you go sweetie pies," instructed Mum. It wasn't long before Zaynab and her two brothers made friends with the other children in the house. There were some from the village, some who had come with Ashraf from London and they also had a few relatives arrive from California, America.

"Welcome, and thanks for coming," greeted Ashraf and politely asked them to take a seat on the sofa.

"Thanks for having us, Ashraf, so what time is the main event happening then?" asked Zaynab's dad.

"Everything will start at one o'clock, we have a couple of hours before the chaos begins," said Ashraf.

"Why don't I show you around the entire house and courtyard, you'll soon get into the wedding spirit if you're not already in it," urged Ashraf.

Over the next few minutes, Ashraf and Zaynab's dad walked around the whole area of the house and courtyard and were quite surprised at the amount of people that were busy preparing and rushing to get the last minute touches to decoration and furniture.

There was a very big arched gate at the front of the main entrance, specifically built to wedding specifications. It was a cultural practice to have the gate built. The wedding gate looked stunning with a variety of coloured dazzling neon lights.

"I'm sure they'll look fabulous when it's dark," said Zaynab's dad.

"Yes, there's a lot of effort gone into that, but I must

say, it does look splendid," confirmed Ashraf.

Both of them strolled through the courtyard. There was a giant tent where all the guests would be having the wedding dinner.

"How many people are you expecting, Ashraf?"

"Erm...I think the entire village will attend no doubt, and there's no stopping the gatecrashers, is there?" replied Ashraf.

"So, that'll be a good few hundred guests then?"

"Yes, something in that region, I guess."

"Well, the tent certainly looks equipped for the numbers, so I wouldn't worry too much, Ashraf." reassured Zaynab's dad.

Both of them moved on towards the back of the house, which was where all the real drama was unfolding. A prominent chef had been hired out to cook the all-important wedding food. The chef was under pressure, although he had several runners assisting him with every detail of the process, from peeling the vegetables, to cutting the chicken and meat to portion size, from mixing the spices to fuelling the outdoor fire that had to be kept going for several hours to keep the giant pots boiling. The giant cooking pots looked like cauldrons and the long wooden spoons appeared like life-size rowing paddles.

"Hello, Sir, How do you do?" greeted the chef in a very polite manner.

"I'm fine, thanks, you seem to have things under control here, then?" Zaynab's dad asked.

"Oh, yeah. Bapu's a great chef, we've looked good and hard to have him come here to cook for the wedding. He's one of the best around," Ashraf interjected.

"Oh, thank you Sir, that's kind of you," replied Bapu.

"So what's on the menu, Bapu?" Zaynab's dad

asked.

"Well, for the starters, I'm cooking Tandoori chicken with my very own recipe, it'll look more orangey, than red, but I assure you it'll taste out of this world, Sir," boasted Bapu. "For the main meal, it's going to be Beef Biryani, with my touch of egg omelette, served with a tender meat curry."

"I feel hungry already, Bapu, it sounds very appetizing and heavenly indeed," Ashraf said. "Have you received the milk order I placed earlier on?"

"Yes, Sir, the milk arrived on time, I am already working on it to make the mouth-watering yoghurt for the dessert, Sir," answered Bapu.

"The traditional homemade yoghurts are one of my favourite desserts, I'm glad you guys chose that," Zaynab's dad said.

"Well, looks like there's a lot to look forward to then," said Ashraf, and they both began to walk off.

Time flew past and the moment had arrived when the guests were filling up the tent. Ashraf quickly rushed inside the house to do last minute checks on everything. He then rushed out and ran over to the tent. All the chairs and tables were nicely in place, all was good to go.

"This is it, the groom's family should be heading our way very soon," muttered Ashraf.

"Yes, it's sort of time for them to come, I guess," indicated Zaynab's dad. "Right Ashraf, I'll leave you to go and receive all your new guests, and I'll just take a seat in the tent with my family."

"Yes, I'll catch up with you later, I suppose," said Ashraf.

"Dad!" shouted Zaynab running in his direction. "We've had so much fun, we've been playing non stop, I've made so many friends and we've been really enjoying spending time talking to the bride," mumbled

Zaynab trying to speak at a hundred miles per hour.

"That's great news. Can you go and find your mum and call your brothers to come inside the tent now please?" requested Dad. And before long, inside the tent was bustling with people, mostly close relatives and friends, eagerly waiting for the arrival of the bride and groom.

The bridegroom had arrived in a traditional *Tanga* with two beautiful white horses adorned elegantly. The *Tanga* halted in front of the barricaded wedding gate, which demanded the groom to pay a fee to gain admission to the wedding venue. This was the custom in many weddings. It wasn't so much a formal event; it was more of a heart warming, good-natured tease of the groom by the siblings of the bride. Moments later, and after a subtle bargain between the gatekeepers and the groom, he was then escorted into the tent like a member of the royal family, and it was another moment where everyone stopped to observe. The groom's dawdling walk made it easy for the camera crew to capture the moment without turning on the slow motion switch. A few steps later, the groom sat down on the royal wedding throne, waiting for the bride to join him.

"Look, Bayyah! There's uncle Ashraf, coming with the bride," shrieked Zaynab with excitement.

"She looks beautiful and her saree looks stunning," Zaynab's mum complimented.

The intricate embroidery made the bridal saree stand out. It was embellished with sequins and minute rubies, making it look ravishing, exquisite and majestic.

"Yeah, I love her saree, Mum, it's gorgeous," Zaynab said.

The bride sat down next to the groom and the pair looked like a match made in heaven. Everything was on track, and the wedding sermon took place almost instantly.

"Let the party begin!" announced Ashraf, and everyone cheerfully rejoiced with the delicious food and drink.

After the wedding feast was over, there was a special time allocated to the bride and groom to get to know the families on the opposite sides. This part of the wedding was largely reserved for close family members. Zaynab's dad had decided to say his goodbyes and called for Ashraf's attention.

"Thank you so much, Ash, we really enjoyed the wedding feast, here's an envelope, it's our gift for the newly wedded couple," beckoned Zaynab's dad.

"Oh, thanks, I'll pass that over to them shortly, and by the way thank you for coming... hope you've had a lovely day... I'll be in touch with you soon," Ashraf promised.

As Zaynab's family began to get in the car, a barrage of fireworks went off in the distance behind them. It was loud and tumultuous but pleasant and exciting. Zaynab's dad looked behind and there was Ashraf there, waving goodbye. He had instructed one of the boys to set off some of the rockets as a token of appreciation. The main fireworks display was reserved for the night. Zaynab's dad waved one final time, and the car drove off towards Budharail.

Chapter Five

Zaynab's Ark

As time passed in the village, Zaynab and her family adjusted more and more to the rural setting. Zaynab's dad had bought a horse. It was a young colt, shiny brown with a distinctive braze white stripe down the middle of the face. It was going to grow into a fine stallion, insisted Zaynab's dad. It wasn't quite ready for running at a Derby, but it certainly met the needs of the children who could ride it lightly across the open plains surrounding the village.

"Dad, why doesn't this horse run?" questioned Zaynab.

"It's only a young horse, it'll slowly learn to do what most horses do. Just enjoy the ride even if it just walks," responded Dad.

It was a good-looking horse, but the children yearned to ride the horse like a real jockey and as it stood, this was not happening.

The days turned into weeks and Zaynab had learnt how to adapt to the countryside very well; that is to say, she learnt all the ins and outs of village survival for a little girl. She was getting good at spotting dangerous creatures in the village. She knew most of the snakes that withered around the riverbed and rice fields near the village. Many were poisonous like the Krait or the Cobra snake, which, although nocturnal, could be seen in broad daylight in many places. She also noted the different types of ants, spiders, bees and mosquitoes that were dangerous to people. Each time Zaynab saw an unusual type of creature, she would look it up and add it to her science fact-finding book, which her dad had asked her to compile.

"Bayyah, it's really amazing how we're getting to come face to face with the world's most dangerous creatures," Zaynab said in fascination.

"Yeah, I love the fact that we're almost like in an amazon forest, but I must admit, it's really scary though," confessed Zaynab's brother.

"You're actually right, Bayyah, if we ever got bitten by any of those poisonous snakes, we'd be dead," cried out Zaynab, with a sudden change of tone from fascination to fear.

"Don't worry Zaynab, they don't tend to come into people's homes. It's by accident that they end up somewhere they shouldn't be. Besides, Dad's said we're quite safe in Budharail as there's been no such incidents of dangerous creatures attacking anyone in their homes."

"Yeah, I'm pretty sure Dad's right because none of the children seem to have said anything about this, I mean, for starters, Dulon would have told us some stories if he knew of any," babbled on Zaynab.

"What makes you suddenly bring up this topic anyway, Zaynab?"

"I saw one of the snake charmers pass by the river earlier today, when I asked who that was, the children told me it was a snake charmer and that he would use his poisonous cobra to entertain people."

"So what's wrong with that?" Zaynab's brother interrupted.

"Well, apparently, if people don't pay him enough money, he sets the cobra on them!" exclaimed Zaynab, gulping in fear.

"Ha, ha!" laughed her brother. "Don't be silly, you're beginning to sound like the village kids," taunted her brother, sounding rather pompous.

"Well, its playing on my mind all day, I could just picture the cobra coming for us," Zaynab murmured.

"Well, you need to start thinking of something else, or else you will be sleeping in fear tonight," expressed Zaynab's brother. Just then Zaynab's dad walked up.

"What are you two jabbering on about then?" he inquired.

"Zaynab thinks a poisonous cobra's gonna come after us," said her brother.

"Well, what makes you think that, my dear?" quizzed Dad.

"Oh, it's nothing Dad, I was just saying there's a lot of dangerous animals and creatures in the village and in its vicinity, that's all," declared Zaynab.

"Oh, well... anyway, I've come to tell you that, the horse will be taken to another village for a few weeks, I have a friend who trains horses for all equestrian purposes. He'll come back more responsive and you can then enjoy riding the horse properly around the village."

"Erm... Dad? What's e-quest-ri-an? Don't think I've ever heard that word in my life," quizzed Zaynab.

"It's a word that means all the things that are linked to horse riding, that's all," explained Dad in the simplest manner. "We need to be able to ride a horse not a donkey. Our horse isn't trained yet, so, that's why it doesn't want to do much," added Dad.

"We've sure got a lazy horse," confirmed Zaynab

with a smug smile on her face.

And in this manner, Zaynab underwent many phases of village life. From snake hunting to horse riding was just the start of her adventurous stay in the village. A further week had passed by and Zaynab's dad was busy planning a trip outside the village. He wanted to make it super exciting and was going to take on a giant project for building a boat. The village was packed with oak trees and hundreds belonged to Zaynab's granddad. It was going to be a boat on a grand scale. Boat building in the village was common, and nearly every household owned a boat, large or small. They were mainly dinghies with the odd ones fitted with an outboard Kubota engine.

With the monsoon season fast approaching, Zaynab's dad thought it was an ideal time to begin the mammoth project of building a boat. The entire landscape of Bangladesh changed in the monsoon season. Rivers overflowed, and great wetlands appeared all over the land. This usually meant a change in the mode of transport from place to place. Everyone would be out on their boats and vessels and Zaynab's dad also wanted to be a part of that scene.

"Children, what do you think about us having a massive boat built for the wet season?" Zaynab's dad asked excitedly.

"That can only be the coolest thing on the planet," shouted Zaynab's brother.

"Dad, that only happens in dreams. Are you serious?" Zaynab excitedly asked.

"Yes, I've been talking to some carpenters and boat engineers, they reckon they can have a fairly large boat built in two months, they tell me it would be suitable for rivers, lakes and even the sea," explained Dad.

"Wow! This is beginning to sound more exciting Dad. What's Mum saying about your project?" Zaynab enquired.

"Well, your mum is fine with the idea. She says as long as it has a suitable lavatory and washroom, it should be okay for all of you."

"Well, then let's go for it Dad, let's build a massive boat so we can have the time of our lives during the wet season," cheered on Zaynab and her brother.

And just like that, Zaynab's dad instructed a team of boat makers to begin the audacious task of building a massive boat from scratch. Over the next few weeks, work underwent on the boat. Hundreds of trees were chopped, skinned and nicely made into planks of wood. The carpenters and boat engineers worked very closely together. One team was going to design the inside of the boat and the furniture. The other team was busy with the actual outward design of the boat and all the safety aspects of it.

There was a great buzz in the village and the word got out about the boat-building project. People from different villages came to see the boat building. It was a new excitement and almost an entertaining platform for the villagers. Women, children, and especially the older men, all flocked to the site each morning and sat in clusters watching every stage of the boat building.

The elders of the village sat with their *Huqqas* puffing away and made it a leisurely pastime to watch. The children collected the wood shavings and spare pieces of wood and played with them in the mini ponds. The women assembled from a distance and watched their children play and admired the talent of the boat builders. Zaynab and her both brothers too joined in, how could they not? This was the most exciting thing happening in the village.

"Zaynab, there's a lot of trees being chopped for this boat, I wonder if it'll affect our oxygen, it looks like we may run out of trees in the village the way we're going!" voiced Zaynab's brother.

"Well, it's only because these trees are quite small, that's why so many are needed," explained Zaynab. "Dad says the boat's gonna take on around a hundred people, and think of the furniture inside, it's all gonna be with wood, so actually come to think of it, what if we run out of trees?" Zaynab questioned.

"Don't worry about running out of trees, there's plenty to go round," said one of the boat builders. "And the oxygen thing, well that's the silliest thing I've heard in a long time, you're worrying for no reason children," he commented with a stern voice.

Zaynab and her brother understood that trees and plants were needed to produce oxygen and clean the air from carbon dioxide. They knew that the more trees that were in a place, the fresher and nicer the atmosphere would be. Both brother and sister were not convinced with the answer from the boat builder, after all he was doing a job and he needed the trees to be chopped to stay in a job. Zaynab and her brother marched back into the house to see their dad.

"Dad, I think we're chopping down too many trees from our village, we may eventually suffocate and die if we run out of oxygen," cried out both of them.

"What on earth have you two been reading and what's brought this on now?" asked Dad, rather baffled.

"The village is beginning to look empty without the trees, there were hundreds and now they're gone, we think something bad might happen to our village," they explained.

"Okay, calm down, let's not get too dramatic now," urged Dad. "If you look carefully, we're only having the oak trees cut down, and yes, it's hundreds of them but, they were planted by your granddad just for this purpose. These are extra trees in the village and they're for this project - so clearly, we're using them," he explained. "And before you say anything else, I am arranging to plant a tree for every one that's chopped down so there's absolutely no reason to worry anymore."

"Hurray!" cried out Zaynab and her brother, with a sigh of relief. They didn't have to worry about the carbon dioxide in the village air anymore.

A month into the project, the massive boat began to take shape. Zaynab's dad decided to make it look like an ark. It was going to have a house-like roof and with several windows on both sides. The house structure was going to sit on the hull of the boat forming the perfect cabin. The front bow of the boat would have carved out verses of the Quran. Layers of beautiful tropical colours of marine paint would be used to decorate the boat; after all, it was costing a lot of money and was a once in a lifetime event, so it had to look good.

The day finally arrived, and the boat was complete. It was now days away from the torrential monsoon rains. The method of launching was going to be a side launch where the vessel would be slid into the water on one side using grease and manpower. The initial boat building happened near the riverside with the intention of an easy launch upon completion. However, the launching wouldn't be done without a grand celebration. The launch date was set for a day in July, when all the rivers and waterways would be perfect for the boat to be launched.

"What a stunning boat this has become, a magnificent job on the ark features, I say," praised

Zaynab's dad.

"It's just so huge and so well built, I love it Dad," joined in Zaynab's brother.

"It's so gorgeous, I can't even believe this is real. It looks a bit like Noah's Ark," complimented Zaynab.

"Well, I wanted it to be outstanding, different and last for a long time to come," said Dad. "It's my first time doing this as much as yours."

"I think we all need to congratulate you Dad, you're so ambitious," praised Zaynab.

"Oh, that's so sweet of you, Zaynab. I've actually decided to name the vessel 'Zaynab's Ark'. We'll travel everywhere on it, and your ark will leave a legacy behind one day," insisted Dad. "After the monsoon rain settles down, with Zaynab's Ark, we'll go on a mighty trip somewhere very far from here."

Chapter Six

A Merry Monsoon

The downpour of the torrential rain began early in the morning. The children in the village ran out to sing and dance in the rain and to celebrate the change in climate. It was in some cases a relief from the baking heat and dusty climate; it provided a chance to enjoy the exotic warm water and lie lazily in the swimming pools. The rivers looked busy with children diving in and out and having great fun, the men tucking up their sarongs and enjoying a nice swim and training their little ones. The women also joined in, and why wouldn't they? They too had been patiently waiting for this season. Their colourful sarees, all dazzling with eye catching floral patterns, could be spotted from a great distance. It was a merry time for all the people in the village; it was once again a merry monsoon.

Unfortunately, there was another face to the eagerly awaited rainy season. With it often came tearing winds with gale force speeds. Riverbanks burst open and flooding in many places was inevitable. Only the higher ground villages remained safe from flooding. Flooding happened every few years but generally the villagers enjoyed monsoons and Zaynab felt lucky when her dad told her that they were in fact on fairly high grounds in Budharail.

"I'm going out in the rain with Dulon," shouted Zaynab's brother.

"Hey, wait for me," Zaynab called.

"Make sure you have a shower after you come back, the rain water is acidic and you need to wash it off," exaggerated Mum. "You'll be drenched with muddy water and dirt too... anyway have fun" she shouted as they left through the front doors.

There was a favourite big pond at the back of the house, where most children gathered and jumped in and out of the water with no worry in the world. Zaynab had taken with her a beach ball and she and her brother went straight to the pond. Soon, all the children were enjoying the thrills of throwing, punching, splashing and catching the ball in the water. They played many different games until they were totally exhausted. Minutes turned into hours but little did the children realise how the time had flown past.

"I love this watar season because we play so much en hav so much fon," said Dulon.

"Yeah, we're having the time of our lives, you're lucky you get this season every year. When we go back to England we'll be missing this so much," said Zaynab's brother.

"You're sure right, Bayyah, I can't think of ever having this much fun in my life, it's so great out here," Zaynab acknowledged.

After a few more minutes, Zaynab's dad walked over to the pond.

"Right, I think it's time to come home, children,

you've had a long day in the pond," reminded Dad.

Zaynab and her brother happily climbed out and quickly ran into the house. They were now starving and wanted to eat something. With all the fun, laughter and jollification, they hadn't realised that they had been in the water for so many hours.

"Mum, what's for dinner today?" asked Zaynab.

"It's duck curry with pumpkin, dear," replied Mum.

"Eww... yuck... I don't like duck," interrupted Zaynab's brother.

"Well, the other option is fabya fish curry with tomatoes," offered Mum.

"I think, I'll choose the fish curry then," Zaynab's brother chose rather unwillingly. The fabya fish, also known as pabda fish, was a type of freshwater catfish with a very delicate texture. It had fewer bones and was suitable for fussy eaters like Zaynab's brother.

"Mum, I love duck, and pumpkin gives it that sweetness. I'll have it any day," Zaynab insisted.

A short while later, Zaynab's family huddled around the dining table to enjoy a freshly cooked duck curry with pumpkin, well, in Zaynab's brother's case, fish curry with tomato.

Each morning it would rain for hours and hours and Zaynab got used to the idea of watching the rain. It wasn't too bad peering at the rainfall; it was soothing and quite relaxing with an aesthetic attraction that drew Zaynab towards it. The heavy pitter-patter, and thudding of rain on the ground released a pleasant and distinctive scent in the air, which inexorably lifted everyone's mood. Zaynab and her brother would sit on the veranda looking out and catching the movements of the tall palm trees, which appeared to be waving at them. The smell of freshly baked peanuts and juicy lychees abetted the pleasure and prolonged the enjoyment. It was a fine lifestyle Zaynab was living; it was a holiday experience that would never be forgotten. Thousands of miles away from the gloomy British weather sat Zaynab enjoying a luxury tropical holiday eating exotic fruits that she had never seen before.

Each day, it was impossible to remain at home while there was so much to explore outside.

"Bayyah, I'm gonna go out now, it looks like the rain has stopped early today," Zaynab announced.

"Yeah, I'll be coming with you...erm...just wait a moment, let me get those fishing nets, it'll be useful to catch frogs with them," Bayyah said.

"Do you wanna call Dulon and a few others, we'll have a nice frog hunting game together," suggested Zaynab.

"That's not a bad idea, let's go," said Bayyah and off they headed out through the doors and towards Dulon's house. Dulon had by now become a very close friend to Zaynab and her brother. He called out a few more of his friends and suggested some good locations to go and play and catch some frogs.

"If we go ovar to the athar side, we will find many many frog there," Dulon said in his broken English. Dulon's English was improving vastly; he could now construct the sentences pretty well, but just needed to work on the pronunciation a little more. And rightly so, he was speaking nearly everyday with Zaynab and her brother and he enjoyed the thrill and challenge of improving his English.

Getting across to the other side meant crossing a *Hakhum*. A *Hakhum* or a *Shaku* was a makeshift bamboo bridge used for crossing small waterways. It stood in between the two villages and they all needed to cross it. The single stretch of bamboo across the small river was only erected in the monsoon and taken down in the dry season. It only had one more piece of bamboo acting as the rail handle to support the crossing. Zaynab and her brother crept vigilantly across the bridge and made it safely to the other side. Dulon and his friends plodded along without any worry in the world.

"Lets go ovar to the frog pond, its always filling with them, thats why its called the frog pond," explained Dulon.

"Yeah, I've got a big jar in my backpack, we can put them all in there," said Zaynab's brother.

The frog pond was a few more meters away from where they stood. The ground had become soft and muddy and it was difficult to trek along the few remaining meters.

"My word! That was a hard venture," shouted Zaynab. "First the bamboo bridge and now through the muddy and wet soil. All to get to this pond hope it's worth the effort everyone." Suddenly, in front of them were many frogs jumping about and going in and out of the pond.

"How do we know which ones are frogs and which ones are toads?" Zaynab asked.

"That's easy, I've looked that up already Zaynab," answered Bayyah. "The short legged and dry skinned ones are the toads, whereas the long legged, smooth skinned, webbed feet ones are the frogs," he explained.

"In that case, I think there's more frogs here than toads, they mostly appear to be smooth skinned with long legs," remarked Zaynab.

"Do you know thet frog legs is very populaar in Bangladesh? So many eating houses cook them and give them to their castomars," explained Dulon.

"Oh, you mean they serve them in the restaurants," clarified Zaynab's brother. "Yes, I've heard the same thing. Frogs and especially frog legs are sold in many places in Bangladesh, they even send them off to other countries," he added. Everyone focused their gaze on the pond.

"These mainly look like Bullfrogs to me. They have that distinctive marking and their feet are webbed," identified Bayyah.

"Wow, look at those tadpoles and froglets swimming around, they look so teeny and sweet," said Zaynab. There wasn't a better time to look for frogs, as monsoon was the frog-breeding season. They were happy with their findings and began catching the ones that looked single and away from the pond. That's only because Zaynab had demanded that nobody caught the mother frogs because she believed the tadpoles and the froglets would be looking for their mummy.

It had been a while since the children had gone out, and Budharail village seemed to be quiet without Zaynab and her brother. They had left in the morning and it was now late afternoon.

"Bayyah, I think we should head back home now, just in case Mum and Dad start looking for us. I mean we didn't really tell them we were coming to this side of the village," implored Zaynab.

"Yeah, I guess you're right. We've caught enough frogs for one day, managed to see so many tadpoles and froglets...yeah let's head back now," agreed Bayyah. "Come on Dulon, let's all get back home now," he instructed.

The team, now happy with their day's adventure, began to trek back towards the bamboo bridge through the muddy and murky waters. They carried a backpack each and had to put their sandals inside it, as they would otherwise get stuck in the mud. They passed by many types of houses; some built with clay with thatched roofs, but more visible were the tin roof houses, which practically dominated the scene. They had just walked a few minutes and suddenly there was a bright flash above in the sky.

"I think we know what that means everyone," shouted Zaynab.

"Let's make a run for it before the rain pounds us," yelled Bayyah. And like a flash of lightning, they ran across the village screaming and yelling, pumped up with adrenaline. But it was too late, the rain had started quite instantly and once more, the heavy thudding rain beat violently on the tin rooftops, creating loud crashing and thumping noises. The rain jostled with the tin roofs recklessly. It looked like the beginning of a monstrous thunderstorm or a cyclone on the way. The tall trees were ferociously shaken as the winds gained momentum. Zaynab and the rest of them could feel the earth trembling beneath them. It was getting dark and foggy and soon it looked like the environment was becoming a harsh and dangerous amazon terrain.

"Run Bayyah! Run!" cried out Zaynab. "Let's get out of here,"

"Yes, Zaynab, we need to make a dash for the house now, before we get blown away," confirmed Bayyah.

By now there was debris being tossed in the air and Zaynab and her friends needed immediate shelter. The water on the ground was quickly rising by the second and suddenly Zaynab and her brother felt scared. They clutched on to each other and stepped gingerly on the semi-flooded ground hoping to get across the dreaded bamboo bridge onto their side of the village.

Dulon was a responsible boy. He made sure he helped Zaynab and her brother cross safely to the other side and then helped one of his friends. He was experienced with monsoon weather and found no obstacles in the whole of the day's adventure. There was a sigh of relief as they made it back to the village in one piece.

"Thanks Dulon, come back for tea after you shower," offered Zaynab's brother.

"Yes, I will," replied Dulon with a big grin on his face.

It was a wonderful monsoon for the children; it provided exploration opportunities and fact-finding missions and expeditions. It was a great time to be outdoors as much as indoors. Zaynab and her brother pulled out their notebooks and began to jot down the adventures they had had. It was indeed a jolly season. For them it was a merry monsoon.

Chapter Seven

The Six Seasons

It was now July, the season was *Borsha,* and Zaynab and her brother loved every bit of the monsoon weather. They had already taken part in many expeditions around the village and experienced first hand the downpour and the relentless torrential rains. They were doing well in their literacy and numeracy lessons at home as the climate provided more opportunity to be indoors than other times. More interestingly though, their science lessons were flourishing. The topic was habitats and they went out on many scientific expeditions to learn about the habitats of frogs, snakes and hundreds of insects. They took a keen interest in science and they knew they were at the right place at the right time and in the right season.

The season *Borsha* also meant the season of some of the favourite fruits of Bangladesh. Mango groves blossomed with ripe and luscious bright orange and yellow mangoes. The jackfruit was the national fruit of Bangladesh and everyone seemed to be keen to point this out. It was enjoyed by all and just one fruit was sufficient for the whole family due to its peculiar size. Zaynab loved the aromatic lychee, which dripped with sweet juice upon peeling them every time. Her brother was fond of the sweet and moist jam, *which* was a distinctively fragrant berry, black on the outside and red on the inside. They were both truly spoilt for choice with all those fruit trees in her granddad's fruit garden and were often surprised to discover some exotic types of fruit which they hadn't even heard of.

"Enjoy the mangoes, berries, and jackfruit while you can," urged Mum. "You won't get the chance to eat them off the trees in England," she said.

"They're also very organic, since they've grown in our very own fruit garden. It's as natural and chemical free as you'll probably get," explained Dad.

"Don't worry Mum, we're sure making the most of it, Bayyah likes the jam fruit so much that he's even chewed on the leaves a few times," revealed Zaynab, trying to suppress her giggle.

"Is that so?" questioned Dad.

"Well, I didn't exactly start eating the leaves! I just wanted to taste it out of curiosity, that's all," explained Bayyah.

"In that case, there's no harm done. Try not to pluck the leaves off any of the plants or trees especially the smaller plants like the sweet and sour *amra* tree, we need them to grow into full trees," demanded Dad.

Zaynab's dad had to emphasise this as he had heard some of the village children had climbed into the fruit garden and ripped *amra* leaves while the plants were at an early and tender stage.

"Don't worry, Dad, my curiosity won't make me do that, I'm a jam and jackfruit fan anyway," stated Bayyah.

"Dad! What comes after this season then?" Zaynab enquired.

"It's the *Shoroth* season, you could say it's equivalent to the Autumn season in England," answered Dad.

"And after that?"

"After the *Shoroth*, comes *Hemontho* a more of a late autumn in Bangladesh. Then you get the *Sheeth* season which is the winter..."

"Does it snow here in winter?" Bayyah interrupted with much excitement.

"No, there's really no snow in Bangladesh, but we do get affected by it from the north of the country. That's where the icy Himalaya Mountains are. When the snow melts there, we get vast volumes of water pouring into the country," explained Dad. "After the chilly Bangladeshi winter, comes the *Boshontho* season which is probably the driest and most convenient time to be here. That's the start of the fun season where *Melas* and funfairs come to life," he continued.

"Wow, that sure sounds exciting. We... are gonna be here for that season Dad?" Zaynab asked.

"Yes, of course, that's the idea of taking a gap year out. It's to enjoy all the seasons and wonders that come along with it. I'll make sure you get to experience the six great seasons of Bangladesh, no doubt."

"That'll be amazing, Dad. We're definitely getting used to staying here. We're getting our schoolwork done on time and I feel I've not missed out on anything school wise," explained Zaynab.

"Yes Dad, I would love to stay here all the way and see all the other seasons. So far, I'm loving every moment," added Bayyah.

"I was thinking you'd benefit from joining the local primary school. Since we're staying for so long. It'll give you the real flavour of Bangladeshi life," suggested Dad.

"Hurray! We don't mind going to school here, now that would be really exciting," cried out Zaynab and her brother.

"So where was I..."

"You were explaining the *Boshontho* season Dad," reminded Zaynab.

"Oh yes, *Boshontho!* It's great in *Boshontho* and most certainly my favourite season. The cars, rickshaws and all the other transport are back to their busy rounds, the weather is great and the days are perfect," he said. "After the *Boshontho* comes the *Grishmo* season, and I'm sure you can guess that we arrived in *Grishmo*-the hot summer, where the heat was scorching and virtually baked us all," laughed Zaynab's dad.

"Yeah, summers here are too hot and sticky, I can't wait for the dry season to come, I want to go to the funfairs and *Melas* that you talked about," shrieked Zaynab with ever more excitement.

"Yes, all in good time children, we haven't fully appreciated the *Borsha* season yet, there's still a lot to do and see with a month still to go, a lot happens here in the wet season," explained Dad.

Just then there was loud screaming and shouting coming from outside.

"What's all the noise about?" asked Zaynab's mum.

"Let me check it out," said Dad and he rushed outside to find out. The more he walked the louder the screaming and shouting became. Zaynab and her brother sneakily followed behind their dad. The noise was muffled and unclear. Zaynab's dad couldn't work out what it was and kept the pace up until he arrived at the main village pool. There were tens of people gathered around the entire area of the pool. Zaynab's dad rushed forward and realised that it was a snake hunt. There was a village myth that if a poisonous snake was touched or chased and failed to be caught the snake would come back to bite the person that night.

A black krait had somehow got into the village pool and the person who spotted it apparently gave it a chase with a paddle, missing it every time. He was frantic and was appealing to everyone to help him catch the snake. He kept on crying out, "The snakes gonna come for me" and pleaded with everyone to help him kill it.

It almost became like a show, everyone was screaming and running every time the snake reached the edge of the pool.

"Hit it with the *loggi*," shouted one man.

"Grab a fishing net," cried out another. The *loggi* seemed ideal for the job. It was a very long sturdy bamboo log used for boat paddling in deeper waters. It was now certainly going to come in use since no one was brave enough to go close to the snake. The snake had become furious and anxious; it speeded from one side of the big pool to the other. Each time it tried to get out on to the bank, the paddles and loggis bashed the poor thing.

"Poor thing," cried out Zaynab. "Why are they trying to kill the poor snake?" she asked her dad.

"Well, lots of strange things happen in the village, dear, unfortunately this has always been the practice here. Maybe if the person hadn't touched it they would have let it go," he explained. "It's because the person touched the snake somehow, he now believes he must kill it."

After a few more minutes one brave elderly man jumped in the water and with one great blow ended the snake's swim.

"Ha ha! A job well done," he shouted in Bangla. "I've done it," he emphasised.

There was relief and the pandemonium subsided pretty instantly. Everyone dispersed and began to head back home as though nothing had happened.

"What drama people create here," said Zaynab's brother.

"I know, they just scream and shout for nothing sometimes," Zaynab replied.

"It's more like they've got nothing better to do, I would say, these things are what makes village life so mysterious," commented Dad. They all headed back to the house and filled in Mum with the dramatic incident.

"Have you both forgot about the big boat your dad had built?" asked Mum.

"You mean, Zaynab's Ark!" Zaynab eagerly corrected.

"Of course we haven't forgotten about it. It's just that every time we went near the boat site, the engineers told us to be patient until the launch day. So we put off any ideas about the boat for a while," explained Zaynab's brother.

"Well, you don't have to put it off for too long now, I can confirm that we will be launching the boat in a few days," revealed Dad.

"I want each season to be marked with an extraordinary adventure, and this season we will be heading far away from here and all the way over to St. Martin's Island," he announced. "Besides, I think it'll do us good to get out of the village for a week or so."

"What a great idea, Dad. It'll be nice to see more of Bangladesh in this season, and we can at the same time test our boat out," said Zaynab's brother.

"Yeah, I can't wait to get on the famous Zaynab's Ark," bellowed Zaynab in her brother's ear.

"You do know it's only called Zaynab's Ark because

it looks like an ark shape and Dad couldn't think of a name at the time!" muttered Bayyah.

And the banter started between Zaynab and her brother, and throughout the next few minutes they debated and taunted each other as they did on many occasions.

Chapter Eight

Stopover, Cox's Bazar

It was early in the morning and it was boat launching day. An invitation had been made to the village dwellers for a celebration dinner at Zaynab's house. Her dad was throwing a party to mark the end of a long and painstaking boat-building period, and also for the successful completion of the entire project. The boat was fully painted with eye-catching colours and the words *'Zaynab's Ark'* were inscribed just under the roof and above the windows on both sides. It was a gorgeous boat, mammoth in size and looked ready to set sail through rivers, lakes, *haors* and the sea.

There was a fairly big tent put up to accommodate the village neighbours and yet again it was another excuse for the poor people to get a good hot meal. A giant pot of fragrant pilau rice and a large pot of goat meat curry were hauled in to the tent as hungry neighbours gathered to eat. As the lids were taken off, the aromatic scent of the saffron in the rice captured everyone's attention, while the steam of the fresh spices in the meat curry teasingly went under their noses.

"I'm so hungry, I can have this whole pot," snapped one of the men, hungry and impatient at the same time.

"Yeah, where's the main man, we need him to come so we can get started," complained another hungry and impatient man.

"I've brought a container with me which I'm gonna fill, if there's any left overs," said a third man.

And on went the neighbours, waiting and counting every second as they waited for Zaynab's dad.

A few moments later, Zaynab's dad walked into the tent.

"I'm sorry everyone for keeping you waiting, I had to make sure everything at the launch site was okay," he explained.

"I thank you all for coming here, and no doubt most of you will join us after the dinner to go and launch the boat in the river," he announced.

"Thank you for inviting us, sir, you are most kind," praised many of the neighbours.

"Well what are you all waiting for? Get stuck in!" ordered Zaynab's dad.

Suddenly the site looked very busy. There was lots of chewing, munching, biting and gulping; it was the sound of eating rice and meat. Hardly anyone spoke to each other for the first few minutes, as they were too busy focusing on their delicious food.

"Oh, I haven't had meat for a long time now, Allah bless this man for providing this opportunity to eat so well," prayed an old man.

"The last time I had a decent meal was weeks back, and that's only after gate crashing a wedding feast, May Allah forgive me, but I was starving," explained another neighbour.

Zaynab's dad could hear these exchanges between the village neighbours and felt a sudden emotion overpower him.

"Oh Allah," he cried out. *"To You belongs all praise, You are the Sustainer of the heavens and the Earth and all that is within them..."* said Zaynab's dad.

After the eating was over, nearly everyone followed Zaynab's dad over to the actual launch site. The boat was on a slipway of logs and one side was facing the river. It was going to be a side launch and Zaynab's dad needed all the manpower to gradually push the giant vessel into the water.

About thirty men, who were muscular and worked in the brick trade, gathered to help get the vessel into the river. They chanted motivational slogans and like a Canto, one person recited and they all repeated after him. Moments later, the beautiful ark-like vessel was launched.

"Glory be to Allah!" shouted Zaynab's dad. "What a smooth operation that was." The buoyancy was perfect; the engineers had done a great job with no flaws. Zaynab's dad was the first to enter the pitched roof cabin. "Smells of timber," he remarked. And no doubt, the entire boat was practically made from timber. "The leather seats and tinted windows all work very well for the interior, I am pleased."

"Hurray!" shouted the engineers, "A job well done I think," expressed the chief.

Zaynab's dad had hired a very capable captain to steer the vessel. "We'll go for a test drive in one of the nearby *haors*," announced Dad. There was plenty of room for everyone, and before long most of the people watching jumped on board. How could they not? It was hard to resist such a once in a lifetime invitation. Zaynab and her brother climbed in too.

"Call Dulon, I don't want him to miss out,"

requested Zaynab's brother. Dulon was also called into the boat.

"Is everyone ready to go?" Zaynab's dad blared out.

"Yes, we're all good to go," came the response from the crowd.

And after a moment of silent prayer, Zaynab's dad instructed the captain to start the engine and to begin the long awaited test drive.

"When we get to the *haor*, I want you to perform all the different manoeuvres and then test the speed to maximum power, I have a great trip planned and don't want to take any chances," explained Zaynab's dad.

"I hear you Sir, I will check and report everything to you Sir," the captain acknowledged.

As the giant, colourful and peculiarly designed vessel passed by the villages, people cheered and waved joyfully with big smiles and amazement. It was an eye-opener for some and a momentous sight for others. People in the boat waved back and joined in. It was somewhat like a jubilee celebration where Zaynab felt like a true princess. The boat gradually began to reach more open waters and the animals, people and houses in the background appeared to be getting smaller. The speed was slowly increasing and suddenly off they went, flying above the water, bouncing up and down at hundred knots per hour. Everyone began to cheer, scream and shout at the top of their voices in excitement. The howling and bawling went on for ages and everyone was having the time of their life.

"I think we'll go as far as *Nullah Haor* and then turn back," suggested Zaynab's dad. *Nullah Haor* was about a two-hour trip at around sixty knots per hour, but this was a test drive time and they had reached there in just under an hour.

"I'm impressed, the vessel seems to perform very

well," declared Dad.

"Yes, Sir. I am very comfortable with all the navigation on this vessel," the captain confirmed.

The test drive had passed with flying colours. Zaynab's dad could now continue and finalise their trip to St. Martin's Island in their new and beautiful vessel. St. Martin's Island, named after a British Governor, was the ideal place to spend a few days away from the village. It was the only coral island in Bangladesh and Zaynab's dad thought it would be fun to explore the island with the family. The first stop was going to be in Cox's Bazar where the longest beach in the world was, and then it was decided that they would visit the island from there. It was going to be by far the most exciting trip up till now. Zaynab couldn't wait and for the remainder of the days she even made a wall chart to tick the days off.

It was a Sunday morning, the first day of the week. The Bazars were bustling with shoppers and fish traders. Zaynab's dad went to fetch some last minute essentials for their mighty voyage to St. Martin's Island. The boat was to leave at exactly eleven o'clock and preparations were underway in the house. Everyone was frantically running around the house trying to get ready. The maids in the kitchen were busy putting together an elegant and exotic last homemade breakfast. It was going to be a fruity one, consisting purely of fresh coconut, banana, mango and seeds of all kinds for the muesli. There were women helping Zaynab's mum pack her suitcase and tidying bits around the room. Some of the friendly neighbours like Dulon came to give Zaynab's brother a hand with his gear and was sad at the fact that he was going to miss them all for a week or more.

"Dad! Can Dulon not come along with us? I'm sure

his parents won't mind," asked Zaynab's brother eagerly. Dulon lived with his parents just a few doors away. His family ran a tiny convenience store in a small hut in the village. His dad was in the shop all the time and it looked quite possible he'd be given permission if he asked.

"Yes, he can come. He can be a useful companion to you and your sister, but first go and quickly ask his mother," requested Dad. "Tell her that I'll take care of his luggage and essentials," he added.

Dulon's mum came running out of the house in tears. "Oh thank you, dear brother, thank you so much for wanting to take my son with you." Zaynab and her brother were confused. Why was she in tears? and why was she thanking their dad, they wondered.

"Not to worry, sister, I will look after him well. He'll be with the rest of them playing and enjoying his time there," Dad promised. Dulon's mum was emotional because she had been unable to give Dulon a holiday since he was born. His parents couldn't afford holidays, not even one inside the country. The thought of Dulon going all the way to Cox's Bazar and St. Martin's Island had overwhelmed her completely.

Finally, the clock struck eleven and it was time to set sail to Cox's Bazar. All the people in the village gathered to catch the sight of the giant vessel leaving the makeshift dock. The anchor was pulled in and the giant boat gently began to move against the mild and sweet breeze.

"Goodbye everyone," shouted the passengers in the boat. The people began to wave profusely and some were even quite tearful.

"Goodbye," they cheered back, smiling and wiping off their tears. And so, off went the vessel steering into the distance, heading first for the district of Sunamganj.

"Shall I run through the route plan, Sir?" the captain offered.

"Yes, of course captain, please do," replied Zaynab's dad.

"We've obviously got a very long route, we'll begin from Sunamganj heading towards Kishoreganj and then to Narayanganj..." began explaining the captain. "From there we aim to cross Chandpur and join the Meghna River in order to pass Noakhali. This is where the trip becomes serious. We will then enter the Bay of Bengal and maybe dock at Chittagong," continued the captain.

"Yes, a stop over at Chittagong sounds most sensible," confirmed Dad.

"From Chittagong, we'll head for Cox's Bazar, again through the Bay of Bengal waters and then from there after our brief stop over we shall sail seventy odd miles and then we should be in St. Martin's Island," concluded the captain.

"I guess, you've planned the route very well, captain," praised Zaynab's dad.

"Not to worry Sir, just doing my job," acknowledged the captain.

After many exhaustive hours of sailing through the water, Zaynab's Ark had now reached the Meghna River, which ultimately flowed into the Bay of Bengal. "Hello, everyone on board," greeted the captain. " We are now currently passing through the Meghna River waters and moving closer into the Bay of Bengal. We will be docking at Chittagong port in a short while." The captain was professional; so far everyone seemed to be enjoying his command and navigation of the vessel. He kept everyone well informed and always kept his focus on the job. He was dressed smartly with a traditional white shirt with four golden stripes on his shoulder boards. His navy blue trouser and captain's hat made him stand out from the rest of the crew.

The vessel entered the shipping lanes and as there were no deadlines for reaching there, it tardily came to a halt. Chittagong was just a brief stop over to purchase fuel and to replenish the food supply. Within an hour everyone jumped back on board the ark and were now happy to sail towards Cox's Bazar.

"Cox's Bazar has the longest beach in the world, can you believe that?" Zaynab's dad revealed with much excitement.

"Wow, that's nice to know. I'm gonna be telling everyone in my class about this when we get back to England," said Zaynab.

"Dad! How long are we staying in Cox's Bazar?" Zaynab asked.

"All depends, Zaynab. We haven't exactly fixed the number of days, but we'll just see how it goes," explained Dad. "If you all really enjoy the beach and the resort we may just stay a few extra days."

Suddenly the microphone on board sounded. "This is the captain speaking, I am pleased to say that we have now reached the shores of Cox's Bazar, please remain seated until the boat comes to a complete stop."

"All praise be to Allah! Great news everyone, looks like our first leg of the voyage was a success," declared Zaynab's dad.

Zaynab and her family disembarked the vessel and headed straight for the resort. About half a mile from the sea beach was Hotel Sea Palace Limited. Zaynab's dad announced that they would check into that hotel.

It was a great voyage so far. The family had seen so much over the long hours of sailing in the sea. They had talked about all the different tourist sites and what to do when they got to each of the places. They enjoyed the swift speed with which the vessel sailed through the waters. They had enjoyed each beautiful river they had crossed. The sunny bright skies pretty much added to the wonderful setting and made it that much more authentic and majestic. They were lucky that no storms were in their path. Zaynab was simply overjoyed with the whole experience and was thrilled with every moment of it. The family and all the rest of the Budharail crew were now fully exhausted. They checked into the hotel and thought the morning would be the best place to start their tour of Cox's Bazar.

"We've had such a good cruise through so many different waters, it's unbelievable," said Dad. "Have you been enjoying yourself, Dulon?" he asked.

"Yes, Ankel. I've really enjoyed the trip so far. To me everything like a dream," he replied.

"Good for you. We'll be going for a meal to the hotel restaurant and after that you can go and have a good rest with all the other kids," explained Dad.

Zaynab's dad had booked a big room for all the kids to crash out in. There was Zaynab and her two brothers, Dulon and three other children that were related to the cabin crew. They were all expected to nestle up in one room as it would be boring for them to sleep with grown ups. This was part of the adventurous planning and made it feel like a real outdoor camping expedition.

Over the next couple of days, Zaynab learnt all about how kind the British Officer, Captain Hiram Cox had been and how he had helped those poor refugee people in that region a long time ago. It was in his honour that the Bangladeshi officials named the market area Cox's Bazar. The old name *Palongkee* was no longer used and it appeared that Captain Cox's generosity had won the day. Zaynab and her family, along with the Budharail crew, visited some Buddhist monasteries and were able to learn some valuable history lessons. Their last day in Cox's Bazar was spent around thirty miles away from the town at the Dulahazara Safari Park, where everyone enjoyed coming face to face with the elephants, monkeys, bears, lions and Bengal Tigers. The sandy beaches were somehow reserved for the trip to St. Martin's Island, and Zaynab's dad had constantly emphasised this point.

"Let's leave the beach parties and sunbathing for when we get to the main place, hey folks," he said. "After all, our main destination is St. Martin's Island," he continued. Zaynab's dad had never been to St. Martin's Island but had been on many occasions to Cox's Bazar. It was as though his heart wasn't in Cox's Bazar and he somewhat hurried everyone to gear up for the main destination.

Chapter Nine

Voyage to St. Martins Island

Zaynab and her family boarded the vessel once again; this time the voyage would be for about seventy miles. The whole trip was to be undertaken through the waters of the Bay of Bengal. Everyone on board had extremely enjoyed themselves for the past few days. Cox's Bazar wasn't bad at all. They had got to do plenty of activities and were quite satisfied with the amount they had covered within the time they had. The ark had one final destination to sail to, and that would epitomise the entire water and beach holiday the family had embarked on.

The day was warm and the sun's rays beat down upon the face of the sea. The skies were crystal clear. There were no signs of grey clouds or anything that would indicate rainfall or a downpour. The water was calm and everyone could hear the birds singing across the sky, high above. The atmosphere was silent, almost too silent for the sea. A mild wind blew in the face of the Captain and Zaynab's dad, enjoying a breath of fresh air outside on the deck. As the boat advanced more and more, only the seagull's squawks could be heard.

"What a perfect day it is, Captain," stated Zaynab's dad.

"Yes, Sir! Enjoy the view all the way to the Island Sir," the captain insisted.

"I'll go in the cabin and join the rest of the them, could I get you some tea perhaps?" Zaynab's dad offered.

"Erm... No thank you Sir, I'm fine," replied the captain.

Zaynab's dad was in the mood for a cup of tea himself. He went inside the cabin and to his surprise saw a pot of tea being brewed. "I was just going to brew up some tea myself," he muttered.

"Not to worry, I was about to send two cups up to you both on the deck," Mum answered.

Zaynab, Dulon and her brothers were all huddled up in front of the laptop playing games. The other three children sat behind them watching in fascination. It wasn't often they saw a laptop or played on such a thing. This was by far a much too expensive luxury for children from the village of Budharail.

As they got further away from Cox's Bazar and into the deeper waters of the Bay of Bengal, the climate began to change quite briskly. In fact the crystal clear blue sky had vanished completely. There were clusters of grey clouds forming and even the sun's rays that had been beating down, began to disappear. The singing birds were nowhere to be heard, the squawking seagulls seemed to have never existed. The mild breeze they had enjoyed began to turn into stronger and noisier winds as it picked up speed.

"There seems to be an abrupt change in the weather, Sir," the captain shouted.

"Yes, I did notice that," answered Dad, "just increase the speed captain and let's sail through as fast as possible... How much distance left, captain?"

"We're more than half way through Sir, I can confirm about twenty miles left, Sir."

"Doesn't sound too bad, okay... maximum speed captain, maximum!" exclaimed Dad.

The vessel now accelerated through the waters with great speed. It bounced up and down as it lifted and dropped against the wavy water. Suddenly raindrops started hitting the giant house-like roof. The sound of the rain got louder and eventually it appeared to be crashing against the roof. It was like bullets hailing down from the sky, the noise became very uncomfortable. The winds now picked up full scale and in the openness of the ocean, the vessel was lonely and entirely exposed. The ark rocked, swayed and tossed violently. It began to shake, wobble and reel dramatically in the turbulent sea. The waves grew bigger in an instant and fiercely pounded against the ark. Zaynab and her family were now caught in the midst of a storm in the waters of the Bay of Bengal.

"Mum, I'm scared," cried out Zaynab.

"This is bad, it's not looking good for us," Zaynab's brother said with a nervous gulp.

"Don't worry children, storms always happen in this part of the country," Mum tried reassuring.

"But this feels really bad, I feel sick Mum," Zaynab cried again, looking through the windows where she could see the monstrous height of the waves.

"Don't look out through the windows, children! Just

close your eyes and hold tight," ordered Mum. Dulon seemed to remain calm as he often did. These things didn't bother him. He was not interested in looking out through the windows nor did he complain about the vessel bouncing up and down and rocking side to side aggressively.

"Everyone, listen very carefully, put on your life jackets and try to stay calm. Please, please don't panic. It might be a violent storm but *InshaAllah* we'll get through it," announced Dad. "You should all pray and remain positive, before you know it, we'll probably be out of the storm."

Zaynab's dad then requested that the captain make an official announcement on the microphone, as he thought it would make the children feel a lot better if the captain spoke to them.

"This is your captain speaking, please note that there is nothing to worry about. I have this boat under control and *inshaAllah* we will arrive at our destination within half an hour."

"See, there's nothing to worry about children, just sit tight," re-emphasised Mum. But the children couldn't really sit tight and just close their eyes and forget about everything. They could feel every little movement and every big turbulent clash of the boat against the sea. They could hear the loud thunder; see the lightning and the terrifying waves. They could hear the ghastly winds and feel the gusts forcefully hitting their boat. They couldn't breathe out of fear and they felt sick to their stomachs. For them, the final half an hour felt like an eternity. Every few seconds they would ask if they had reached the shore.

The storm was indeed violent and for a long few minutes even Zaynab's dad began to worry about the outcome. They were well equipped, but this was

Bangladesh. Would the rescue services be able to come in time? Was there such a service in the first place? He wondered. All he could do was just pray to Allah and hope for the best possible outcome.

"Everyone, please join me in the prayer," he ordered. Zaynab's dad offered a silent prayer, he prayed and prayed and it seemed to go on forever. No one minded this. He didn't look left or right and remained heavily absorbed in his silent words. Suddenly the pelting rain subsided. The crashing noise against the roof began to fade away. The violent rocking became serene and gentle sways that felt more soothing than anything else. The mist and fog cleared up and the grey and dull sky lit up and it appeared that the sun suddenly began to listen to the prayer and beat down its rays to its full capacity. By then the vessel had reached the shore of St. Martin's Island.

"All praise be to Allah and Glory be to Allah!" cried out Zaynab's dad. Everyone joined in without hesitation and agreed.

"What a relief! The end story could have been bad today," uttered Zaynab's brother.

"Yes, Bayyah. We've made it safely. I can still picture the tall waves though. But I'm glad we've made it," shouted Zaynab.

"Thank you captain, you did a marvellous job," praised everyone.

Everyone's mood changed rapidly, the smiles and laughter came out once again. The excitement and holiday mode was switched on one more time. They had reached the Island safely, unscathed and in high spirits. It was now time to check in the hotel and relax, it was a time to take a fresh breath of air and look forward to the next few days of sun, sand, water and fun.

Zaynab's family checked into the Blue Marine's Resort hotel. It was a luxurious hotel with fully furnished rooms and beautiful scenic views from each room. The calm blue ocean lay in full panoramic view and the birds hovering above the beach made an entertaining sight to watch.

That night everyone, including Zaynab, slept like a log. And who could blame them? They had had a frightening ordeal that would be remembered for a long time to come.

It was the break of dawn and the roosters could be heard crowing all over the Island. It was not the most pleasant sound to be jolted awoken with, but it certainly reminded everyone where they were.

It was the second day on the Island and today was going to be an exploration day, thought Zaynab. She quickly jumped out and began to wake everyone else up. Her brother had missed the rooster's crowing and he slept through it, virtually oblivious to its existence.

"Wake up Bayyah, wake up!" Zaynab beckoned.

"What time is it?" Bayyah asked.

"Never mind the time, Bayyah just wake up, it's time to wake up. It's actually breakfast time," Zaynab repeated. Dulon was right besides Zaynab's brother and he quickly jumped out of his bed not knowing the time or why he was woken up.

"Let's all go down and have breakfast, I've already seen Dad downstairs at the breakfast table," said Zaynab.

Moments later, everyone was gathered round the breakfast table in the hotel restaurant, ready to have their first breakfast on the island.

"Yummy, I'm having that parata with omelette," shouted Zaynab's brother.

"I'm having the same as you Bayyah, What do you

want Dulon?" Zaynab kindly asked.

"I'll have the parata with daal and a little bit of that vegetable curry please," Dulon requested.

"Hey! Your English is really getting good now Dulon, looks like you've improved a lot," remarked Bayyah. It was a jolly time around the table and Zaynab enjoyed the delicious Bengali traditional breakfast. After munching on the tender and soft paratas and finishing their mouth watering breakfast they slowly began to make their way outside in the bright open daylight.

There was a large placard further away from the hotel and Zaynab was curious to know what it read. She walked over to it and discovered it was written in big Bangla letters. Zaynab called her dad over and asked him to read the sign for her.

"My dear, the sign reads, 'Narikel Jinjira' which simply means Coconut Island," Dad explained. And indeed it was a coconut Island, everywhere Zaynab turned there were coconuts, which reminded her of the coconut trees back in the village.

It was a pleasing sight to see so many fishing boats all in different shapes and sizes. Some were without engines and with just a paddle on them. Zaynab was told that the Island's people lived on a fish diet and it was very important they had these boats going out every single day. Further up the Island, Zaynab and her crew noticed an abandoned turtle hut. They couldn't understand why no one was there to look after this hut and through the creaky wooden doors they could see empty cages lying all across the floor. However, Zaynab did see lots of turtles near the beach. She saw large and medium as well as small and tiny ones. She loved every minute of it.

"Oh wow, they look so adorable, especially the baby

ones," she praised. There were plenty of turtles crawling around. "I wish I can take one with me back to the village, especially that baby one," she hoped.

Accompanied by her Dad, they all got on a small dinghy to explore the blue water. They could see only glimpses of stunning coral wherever they turned. "It would take a deep scuba dive to appreciate the wonderful colours of the vibrant coral reef," said Dad. After all, the Island was known for its coral reef and was the only one of its kind in the country.

"Zaynab! Did you know that the corals are marine animals?" Dad asked. "They actually catch tiny fishes."

"That's amazing, you couldn't easily guess that without learning about them," she muttered in fascination.

They calmly paddled around the still blue water, taking in the breathtaking views and enjoying the delightful warm breeze. It was peaceful and the feeling was unbeatable. They rocked the boat on purpose and enjoyed the splish-splosh that it created. Zaynab's dad scolded at first for rocking the boat but then joined in himself. It was so funny that Dulon laughed till he fell off the boat. They all paddled back to the shore, only to see Dulon beat them back because of his fish-like swimming ability. Dulon was bred in Budharail where it was almost like an unwritten rule to be a good swimmer. With a popular river flowing through the village it was a trendy hotspot for Budharail kids to master their swimming.

Zaynab's exploration day was now fully underway; she and her crew had already covered vast portions of the Island. They were free to roam around and explore the Island. They passed the fishing boats and saw all the different types of fish being pulled in. They dared each other to touch crabs and stroke the giant squids and lobsters that the fishermen brought in. They picked up baby turtles and then dipped their toes in the beautiful blue ocean waters. All along Zaynab's dad made sure he was keeping an eye out. It was his responsibility to make sure Dulon was enjoying himself but was safe from any harm. Zaynab and her brother didn't know how to swim properly, they were forbidden to enter the ocean above knee level unless an adult supervised them.

"Bayyah! Did you notice that, there's no electricity on this Island. Dad told me that only the top hotels use generators to power up," Zaynab commented.

"Yeah, I've noticed that there's no cars, or motorbikes on this Island. There's only rickshaws, that's about it...and obviously boats." Zaynab's dad walked over to them.

"Looks like you lot are really enjoying this tour on the Island, I know I'm loving every minute of it," said Dad.

"Yes Dad, it's the openness, the water, the boat rides and the fact that we can play with our ball all day long on the beach. We're absolutely loving it," they confirmed.

They all walked together chatting and giggling. They passed an almost rotting and ramshackle hut from which heavy steam was belching. It was a tea stall, brewing fresh tea.

"Just on this occasion, why don't you all join me for a cup of tea?" requested Dad.

"That's a first!" muttered Bayyah. Zaynab and her brother were not normally allowed to drink tea until they were a bit older.

"Yeah, go on Dad, let's all have tea together then," Zaynab, agreed.

They all sat down on the clear sandy beach, each with a cup of tea in their hands. They glanced around the entire Island and wondered how calm and serene it looked. The voyage to St. Martin's Island had been a great success. It had been the best trip for Zaynab and her family so far; it was adventurous and full of mystery. No two days were the same and Zaynab could only thank her dad for planning such an exemplary voyage. It was a voyage to explore the beautiful coral Island that offered so much peace and serenity and so much joy and happiness. It was no doubt a coconut Island and Zaynab felt that the words 'Narikel Jinjira' were now imprinted deep into her heart.

Zaynab knew that the voyage to St Martin's Island was not going to be topped by any other trip no matter how long she lived in Bangladesh. This was the only trip that had taken months to prepare from the building of the ark to waiting for the right climate. The travel through the turbulent sea made it all the more memorable and the experience now became significant and necessary to share with everyone, she thought. "What a nice story I'll be able to tell my friends when I get back to England," she muttered quietly. "The storm and the panic we had will be something I won't forget easily."

St Martin's Island felt like home. Although her stay on the Island was brief it felt like weeks as she covered one end to the other practically each day. With no hustle and bustle and noisy bazaar type atmosphere, Zaynab made the most of her pleasant time on the Island.

Chapter Ten

Jonota Market

After another couple of days, Zaynab and her family returned back to Budharail in the mighty vessel. This time they had escaped any storms and were glad to be home without a dramatic encounter with the weather. All the people in the village had gathered waiting their arrival and it almost felt like they had been gone for months.

"Oh yes! Home sweet home," burst out Zaynab's brother.

"Yeah there's no place like home, I can't believe we're back to Budharail again," voiced Zaynab.

"All thanks to our captain, we've arrived much faster than planned," said Dad. "He sure is a good captain. He never panics and always stays focused behind the wheel."

The captain had joined them all the way to the

village home and was invited in for tea. He was from Sylhet and was going to return after Zaynab's dad had finalised his wages for the whole journey.

"I am delighted you've stopped by captain," said Dad. "Just wanted to say how much we enjoyed the trip and your professional assistance throughout the whole voyage. We really did depend on your expertise out there in the storm."

"Like I said, Sir, I just happily do my job, please be in touch if you need me again," he offered.

"I shall be in touch captain. I most certainly will, besides you, I wouldn't have anyone else control that vessel," confirmed Zaynab's dad.

"I have actually decided to put the vessel up for sale before we part for England, obviously the inscriptions on the ark needs to be erased, but I think everything else is pretty much in excellent shape," Dad revealed.

"I know many people in the business who may be interested Sir, I will spread the word at once and will be in touch if something comes up," assured the captain.

"Very well."

The captain said his goodbyes and waved to the whole family before he leaped into his very own speedboat, which was securely parked for him during his leave.

Zaynab was quite happy to be back in the village, not because she hated the recent trip but solely because it was the end of many sleepless nights and exhaustion from travelling. She really enjoyed the village life because she could be out with her brother and her friends the whole day and come back to a lovely spacious home with hot home-cooked meals ready to eat.

"Tomorrow is Sunday, and that means it's the village market day," announced her dad. "We need to go and do a big shop as it looks like we're low on everything."

"Yeah that sounds great, I can't wait to check those bats out again," shouted Zaynab.

The village market was once known for its countless bats. Among the tall trees surrounding the village were hundreds of bats making their home in the tree hollows. They had been living there for years, roosting from pup to adulthood. The market was even named after the bats for a number of years before it took on a more suitable name, the Jonota Market, which meant the public market. Zaynab's dad remembered his childhood visits to the village bazar and recalled how the bats usually hung upside down with their wings tightly furled around their bodies.

"Did you know that the village market was once called the 'Badurer Bazar', meaning 'The bazar of bats'," said Dad. "It's because of the number of bats that used to be there, it appeared at one stage that the bats almost infested the bazar. However, it's much calmer now, and the bats you see now are nowhere near what used to be there a long time ago."

"It's probably because they've chopped down the tall trees and got rid of the deserted buildings," suggested Zaynab's brother.

"Yes, it could be due to that, or it could be because people have hunted them down," said Dad.

"Well they could have possibly migrated as well," Zaynab suggested.

It was an interesting topic because bats were fascinating mammals and it fitted very well with Zaynab's habitat topic in science.

The next morning, Zaynab was jolted awake by the sound of the cockerels.

"Cock-a-doodle-do!" Went off the clamoured sound.

"Oh god, not again," she moaned.

"Cock-a-doodle-do!" Sounded another rooster and at this point Zaynab thought it was a good idea to get out of bed. The morning was nice and bright and the air was warm but not humid. Birds were chirping in the distance. Zaynab could hear ducks quacking and could make out that a mother duck was leading her raft of ducklings around the block. There were many things going on in the morning, for instance the fishermen. They were out very early and now returning home with their mighty cheerful catches. The whole animal kingdom also seemed to get busy around the village on a mission to find food.

The smell of freshly cooked vermicelli in sweet creamy milk and cinnamon filled the stairways. After getting ready, Zaynab rushed to the dining room downstairs to join her family for breakfast.

"Oh, I enjoyed that," called out Zaynab licking every last bit off her bowl.

"Yes, I can see. Your dish looks washed already, good for you!" Dad said.

"Yeah, I enjoyed that pudding thing too, and I loved the soft almonds," said Bayyah.

"It's called *shemai*," Mum pointed out.

"Yeah the *shemai* was great," repeated Bayyah.

"Okay, children. It's time to get ready to go to the bazar, it's market day today!" Dad reminded everyone.

After another rushed few minutes Zaynab and her brother headed to Jonota Market with their dad.

Jonota Market might have been small but it had every type of shop that a village could wish for. It appeared that the market was divided into two main sections. There were rows of permanent shops facing each other and in between were temporary day trading stalls, which would disappear at the end of the market day. It was breathtaking seeing the different types of buying and selling that was going on. It was a cramped market with busy, bustling people in every corner.

Zaynab walked passed the main row of shops.

"Bayyah, you count the right hand side shops and I'll count the left hand side," demanded Zaynab.

"Ok, I'll go first, I can see a pharmacy, a pottery store, barbers, blacksmiths, a grocery store, a book store, tea huts," said Bayyah.

"Right I can see, a furniture shop, a laundry, a sweet shop, some more tea huts, a mobile phone shop, a jewellery shop and a clothes store," confirmed Zaynab.

"Wow, you both are learning a lot about the market shops, I may as well join in your game too," Dad insisted. "I can see small stands with meat and poultry on banana leaves, baskets of dried fish, and rows of fresh fish. Ducklings and chicks for sale, egg stands, stands for green and yellow betel nuts peeled and unpeeled, finely chopped and whole. There's also a fruit stand and a vegetable stand, actually far too many to count... a peanut and Bombay mix stand and a frying stand too, and look, there's a handy sugar cane stand as well," gasped Zaynab's dad as he said everything in one breath. "Let's go over to the sugar cane stall first," suggested Dad. The freshly displayed sugar cane juice was simply irresistible.

"We'll have three full glasses, please," requested Zaynab's dad.

"Yummy, that sounds nice," said Zaynab.

The three of them moved around the bazaar and went to shop after shop, carefully selecting all the goods they needed. The wonderful rows of colourful vegetables and fruits were breathtaking. Zaynab noticed so many types of Desi vegetables. Stacks of bright green bottle gourds, known as *Louw*, heaps of bitter gourds known as *Kerela*. Green papaya, peas, runner beans, cucumber, snake gourds, Basil, okra, spinach, ridge gourds, balsam apple, asparagus bean, lime and coriander and green chillies were all lined up in one row. It was fascinating to see because all these vegetables were the same green colour.

"These vegetables look so stunning, but I don't know half of their names," Zaynab shouted.

Zaynab's dad pulled out his mobile phone and took a snapshot of the mouth-watering vegetables.

"There you go, we'll go over the names at a later time, maybe when we get back to the house," he said.

Zaynab now looked curiously at the rows of fruit. Again these were exotic and Desi. Mangoes, Lychee, Jackfruit, Carambola, berries, custard apple, palms, coconuts, acid fruit, pomegranate, guava, pomelo, star apples, hog plums, wood apples, olives, grapefruit, tamarind bunches and lotkons were all on display.

"Dad! Photo time!" she instructed.

Zaynab's dad was happy to take another snap shot of the fruits; after all, it was going to aid the process of learning for Zaynab and her brother. Moments later, they stopped at the sweet stall.

"Nice hot *jilebi*, very hot *jilebi*, sweet tasting *jilebi*," chanted the seller with the most obnoxious tone.

"He's trying so hard, maybe I'll just get a little bite size, just to keep him sweet!" grinned Dad. And rightly so, the hot steaming sweet *jilebi* was so tasty that Zaynab's dad asked for another big batch to take home for later.

The bustling market was in full swing and they all began to speed up their shopping as it was getting late. Zaynab's dad now stopped at the fish stalls.

"What shall we have tonight for supper?" he asked

"Erm...those king prawns look tasty," answered Bayyah.

"Yeah, king prawns Dad! Let's get king prawns," Zaynab repeated.

"We'll have two kilos of king prawn please," requested Dad.

"What shall we have the king prawns with, any ideas?"

"Erm...let's have them with spinach," said Bayyah.

"With small potatoes," shouted Zaynab.

"How about if we had it as a king prawn biryani?" suggested Dad.

"We'll go with that any day," replied Zaynab and her brother.

Suddenly, everyone was shaken by the sound of the *Adhan*, it was the call to the afternoon prayer. All the shops began to close one by one but this would be just until their prayers were done. Zaynab's dad quickly arranged the delivery of the shopping with one of the shop owners and headed for the village mosque, which was en route to the house. After about fifteen minutes, the three of them continued back towards the house. It was an exhausting few hours, moving from shop to shop in the busy marketplace, but it was thrilling and fascinating for Zaynab, as she learnt a lot about the village Jonota Market and very much enjoyed the wonderful village shopping experience. The crowded atmosphere and the dazzling colours in the different shops, the fragrance of fruit and the scent of outdoor frying captured Zaynab's senses. The market was not only just a learning place; it was also a place where Zaynab felt really happy.

Chapter Eleven

The Friday Auction at the Mosque

The mosque was a central focal point of village life. It was where hard working labourers got a break and could sit together praying and meditating in peace. It was also a place where the men could escape to and assemble for a brief chatter after prayers. The village mosque was, however, in a poor state - it was just about held together with bamboo canes and had a thatched roof made of grass and hay. The flooring was a mixture of silt, sand and clay and it didn't hold together too well in each monsoon downpour. It was small and Friday prayer gatherings made it appear to be crammed, jammed and overcrowded. There was an open area near the mosque known as the *Eidgah*. It was where the Imam of the mosque delivered the Eid sermons and the openness was meant to create a warm community spirit as well as provide a more capacious area.

Zaynab's dad attended regularly and regretted the fact that the mosque was in such a predicament. He thought hard about how he could help and came up with a fantastic idea for raising funds so that the mosque could be perhaps rebuilt or at the very least get refurbished.

"Children, you know I'm ambitious about starting mighty projects, and as I've demonstrated with Zaynab's ark, anything is possible here," declared Zaynab's dad. "This time my project, my goal and aim, is to have the village mosque totally transformed."

"What do you mean, Dad?" Zaynab enquired.

"I am going to raise funds and with the help of the whole village, try to rebuild the mosque to a very good standard. I have a great idea about a Friday auction that I'm going to introduce, obviously with the approval of the Imam, and I'm hoping within a few months we'll have enough funds to start the work," explained Dad.

"That's a great idea, Dad, but what type of auction are you thinking of?" Zaynab's brother asked.

"The auction could be to sell anything from clothing to food. Even livestock could be included as long as people give a description of their animal and its weight. As they'll use the mosque platform to get a good sale they'll be required to donate, let's say fifteen percent of their sale price to the mosque..."

"That percentage sounds a little low, it might take a while before lots of money rolls in," Zaynab's brother commented.

"You haven't let me finish yet...I am also proposing to have a one month period where people donate furniture and all types of goods to the mosque. The donations can even expand beyond our village, I am positive hundreds of items will be pouring in as donations and you know what comes next...?" He quizzed.

"Yeah, you're gonna then auction all those items and

raise hundred percent for the mosque! Wow nice plan, Dad, really great idea," shouted Zaynab's brother.

"Yeah, cool idea Dad," Zaynab praised.

"We will begin this noble project by donating as many goods as possible from our own house. I am also going to ask the skilled women of the village to weave bamboo slats into baskets and hand fans and other useful items. I will provide as much bamboo as they need,"

"Way to go, Dad! I can picture the whole house filling up with bamboo items!"

"This is yet another exciting time for us, it'll be so fun raising this money and then watching the mosque being re-built. I can't wait to start," shrieked Zaynab with excitement.

Zaynab was so proud of her dad. He had yet again come up with a great project that was not only fun and enjoyable, but which kept Zaynab and her family involved, busy and absorbed in the village life. She muttered to herself, "The horse was fun, even if we had to sell it off that soon. The ark was an out of this world experience, and now this re-building mosque thing sounds even better. Oh, I do love this village, always something great happening here. "

It was now the *Shoroth* season, early autumn, and the harvest festival was underway. It was a great time for Zaynab's dad to roll out this project. People could donate crops, rice, flour, wheat and all the many ripened and lush fruit and green vegetables that they farmed. It was an idea that opened up interesting doors for all the people in the village. The men and women could get involved in many different ways. Those who couldn't donate anything could help in the making and weaving, cleaning and dusting. There were skilled women in the village who could hand craft fancy bamboo items and who would be grateful to help. The atmosphere in the village was absolutely electrifying. Everyone welcomed the idea and began to talk about how they could get involved.

Zaynab's dad arranged an appointment with the Mosque Imam to share his passionate ideas about his latest project on the village mosque. Without doubt, he received the Imam's approval.

"I have one rather urgent request though," said the Imam.

"Yes, go on."

"It's about my house. You see I'm from Mymensingh and my family home is situated near Durgabari Road, fortunately we've been offered a good sum of money for selling my house as it falls in a busy shopping location. Erm..." hestitated the Imam. "I was wondering if I could relocate to Budharail and live here with my family," asked the Imam.

"I can't see a problem with that Imam Sahib, but where exactly do you plan to move into?"

"That's the thing, Sir, I was thinking... Erm..." hesitated the Imam again. "If I could perhaps temporarily move into your bungalow in the fruit garden, Sir,"

"I'll have to think about that Imam Sahib, I'll let you know tomorrow," Zaynab's dad stated.

Zaynab's dad thought long and hard about Imam Sahib's request. He'd be a good person to occupy the bungalow, he thought. However, Zaynab's dad had a request to make himself. If the Imam agreed, then he would have no problem giving the Imam the bungalow. The next day, Zaynab's dad went over to the Mosque to meet Imam Sahib.

"I have given your request good thought, and I'm pleased to say that you can move into the bungalow and call your family over here from Mymensingh, but only on one condition, Imam Sahib," Zaynab's dad proposed.

"What's that, Sir?"

"I need you to teach Bangla to my children, I'll pay you of course, but it needs to be thorough and regular tuition," insisted Zaynab's dad.

"With pleasure Sir, with absolute pleasure," Imam Sahib repeated.

"Okay, now that's out of the way, shall we continue with the expansion of the mosque and the fund raising plan behind it?" suggested Zaynab's dad.

"Yes, I think so. Indeed we shall," replied the Imam with a huge smile on his face.

And so Imam Sahib and Zaynab's dad talked at great length, discussing all the possible options to bring in the money for rebuilding the mosque. On that particular Friday, Imam Sahib mentioned in his sermon the need for funding and kindly asked everyone to put their heart and soul into the project. It was going to be a community project and a reason for bringing together everyone in the entire village. Everyone came out with a buzzing mind, energised and full of motivation to get the project rolling. So over the next few weeks the whole village got together and carried out their roles. The women got busy with the bamboo slats; the carpenters and the skilled craftsmen came together to make various pieces of wooden furniture. The children became helpful by being runners and assistants for their parents. It was quite a buzz in the village, all working for a common goal.

"Dad, when is the first auction?" Zaynab asked.

"It's next Friday, straight after the *Jumma* prayers," Dad answered. "It will run for many weeks, and the items that don't shift, we'll sell off in the Sunday bazar each week," he explained.

"That's excellent Dad, that means we'll reach more people."

"Yes that's exactly the idea, Zaynab."

That Friday as planned; Imam Sahib stood up and announced the opening of the first auction. Everyone cheered excitedly and the auction got underway. Zaynab's dad was one of the Auctioneers alongside Imam Sahib. It was great fun for Zaynab and her brothers to watch, it was hilarious seeing their dad call out and describe the different items.

"We have here a beautifully decorated bamboo vase, hand crafted with the finest talent, I am opening this at hundred takas..." Zaynab's dad broadcasted.

"One Twenty," shouted a member of the crowd.

"One Forty," shouted another. And very quickly a third man shouted, "One Sixty." For a short moment no one else bid.

"One Sixty, going once, One Sixty going twice and One Sixty going..."

"One Eighty," interrupted another voice. Zaynab's dad looked around the room. He had missed the person who'd shouted it.

"Who's shouted One Eighty, please show your hand," he insisted.

"Yes, it's me, One Eighty from me," said the man. It was Dulon's dad. He'd just stepped into the room and made the bid.

"Okay then, One Eighty going once, One Eighty going twice... and One Eighty going thrice...sold!" Zaynab's dad declared as he struck the gavel on the wooden sound block.

"Bayyah, this is fun. Look at Dad, he's enjoying

himself at the front, he's just sold the first item of the day."

Zaynab and her brother watched with amazement. The auction was buzzing with people and they were genuinely interested in helping out the mosque. Zaynab's dad's idea was going to be a great success. Over the next few weeks, many products and items were brought over to the mosque. People from many different villages came forward to help the cause and Zaynab's dad was busy flogging the goods off one at a time. After a long month of painstaking selling and encouraging people to donate, Zaynab's dad and the Imam Sahib, alongside one or two of the mosque committee members, sat down counting all the money they had accumulated.

"Imam Sahib, so what's the total coming in at?" Zaynab's dad asked.

"It looks like we've hit forty-five thousand takas."

"That's not bad at all, that's great news. We can safely start the work and hopefully continue to raise more funds," Zaynab's dad said.

"We need about ninety thousand takas to a *lakh* to complete the entire work," said one of the members.

"Yes, we'll be able to get half of it done with what we've raised, but we still need to raise another similar amount," said the other member in the meeting.

"Okay, let's not worry about the remainder of the funding, I'll make some calls back to England and I'll see if some of my friends would like to help our cause," Zaynab's dad stated. "I can't promise the full sum but I'll certainly try my best to get some help."

The faces of Imam Sahib and the two members lit up, they were very pleased to hear Zaynab's dad's offer to stretch out to England. After all, in England was where all the money was, they thought.

A few more weeks later, Imam Sahib stood up to deliver his weekly sermon on Friday. He thanked everyone for their support and then announced the greatest news that anyone in the whole village would ever hear.

"All praise be to Allah, we have most certainly reached our target, and we now have the full amount of funding to carry out the rebuilding of the mosque. Thanks to the Friday auctions we have now found a new system of raising money," Imam Sahib announced. The congregation went ecstatic and everyone began to embrace each other in joy and happiness. They were finally going to have a bigger, better and a newer mosque and it was all down to Zaynab's dad's idea of starting the Friday auctions.

"What a great idea this action turned out to be," voiced Zaynab and her brother.

Chapter Twelve

The Queue at the Clinic

Time passed and it now moved from the season *Shoroth* to *Hemnotho,* where the late autumn blooming flowers blossomed and the soil became fertile once again after the long stretch of being buried under water. Zaynab had witnessed many seasons and had enjoyed the mouth-watering variety of exotic fruits that came with each one. As the fields became drier, they began to fill with lush green grass. The cows, goats and sheep could be seen grazing away on the rich and luxuriant pastures. The cats and dogs chased the raft of ducks and the clutch of chicks. Cockerel fights took place around in the different parts of the village. It was a nice feeling to be able to walk on those places, which were before submerged in water. However, there were the small crater-like dents in the ground all over, which held patches of muddy water, which hadn't yet dried out.

One morning as Zaynab was walking across the open plain in front of the village swimming pool, she suddenly dropped her bracelet in one of the small craters.

"Oh, great! I can't even see where it's gone in this thick mud," she muttered. She picked up a branch that was lying by and gave a big stir in the puddle of muddy water, trying to see if she could locate her bracelet. But she had no luck. "I'd better get in the muddy pothole and check with my own hands," she tutted. She spent quite a long time trying to sieve through the mud in order to find her bracelet.

"Ah ha! There it is, I can feel it," she gasped. And rightly so, she had managed to pull out her bracelet without much trouble. Zaynab's hands and feet where now fully plastered in mud. But this didn't matter as she walked away with her missing bracelet.

Suddenly Zaynab felt a tingling sensation in between her toes on her left leg.

I wonder why my toes feel like that, she thought. She looked carefully at her toes wiping off the dense muddy water and was horrified to discover that a leech had bit her foot in between her toes.

"Heeelp!" Zaynab cried out. "Heeelp!"

Someone nearby quickly came to Zaynab's rescue. "What is it, dear girl? What's troubling you?" asked the old man.

"There's a big leech stuck in between my toes and I'm too scared to take it off," Zaynab whimpered.

"Right, don't panic dear, I'll have it off your foot in a flash," the old man said. And before Zaynab could breathe, the old man pulled off the big leech and threw it across the field. Zaynab's foot was now bleeding. The leech had managed to suck a bit of blood and as it was pulled off vigorously it left her foot a little sore.

Luckily, right in front of Zaynab was the village

clinic. It was a clinic that provided minor surgery and there was a doctor available to check people's illness and wellbeing. Zaynab quickly made a dash for the clinic to show the doctor her bleeding foot.

As she went round the entrance side, she could see a big queue of people waiting for their turn to see the doctor. Zaynab tutted again. "I'll never be able to see the doctor in time, this queue is gonna take all day," she said, rather frustrated.

She quietly walked over to the queue and went straight to the back and patiently lined up.

The village clinic was a free clinic, a little bit like the NHS service in England. But in Budharail there was an unwritten rule about who used the clinic. It was a general belief that people who could afford private health care stayed away from the clinic, that is to say, they were expected to pay for their service at a private clinic. Some poor people from other villages also came to the Budharail clinic and Zaynab could tell this as she hardly recognised anybody in the queue.

"What is that girl doing here in this queue?" moaned one of the women in the queue. She was holding her child, who was perched on her hips. She wore a very old saree with several patches that you could tell were hand stitched unscrupulously.

"Yes, she comes from that *Haji Bari* behind that fruit garden, she shouldn't be lining up here," said another woman.

"She can afford to go and see a private doctor. Looks like she wants to take advantage of the free service here," said the woman with the child, smirking at the same time.

These women were strangers to Zaynab and she couldn't figure out why they were jibing at her sarcastically. She ignored them and patiently continued to remain in the line.

By now the line had moved up and there were only a few more people left in the queue. New people however joined behind Zaynab and the process continued. The doors to the doctor's room were wide open. Zaynab could see and even hear what the doctor was saying to the patient inside the room.

"There's no privacy here," she muttered loudly.

"Well what do you expect here, if you want privacy, you can go and pay for a private doctor," said the voice behind her.

By now Zaynab had become furious. She needed to correct some of those rude people in the queue. They were being nasty to her without her having done anything wrong. She thought to herself what was bothering those people? It wasn't as though she was pushing in the queue or robbing them of their turn. She needed to find out why these people were making such remarks. Zaynab took immediate action. She moved out of the line, walked passed the two women in front of her and barged into the doctor's room with an abrupt force. She went right in front of the doctor and complained.

"Those horrible people out there are saying nasty things about me, doctor, I want you to have a word with them," Zaynab demanded.

"What's the matter dear, have you been hurt or injured or something?" asked the doctor.

"Some of those people out there are saying I shouldn't be here, this is my village and this is our village clinic and I'm sure you don't mind seeing anyone doctor," Zaynab jabbered on.

By now the doctor realised that Zaynab was

probably in the queue. He smiled and consoled her.

"What's your name dear?" asked the doctor.

"My name is Zaynab, Zaynab Islam," she replied.

"Well, Zaynab. Take no notice of those people outside. They're from really poor families and they often take it the wrong way when they see people from England come to these clinics. They don't understand that we receive a lot of funding from families like yours," explained the doctor. "Please don't take any notice of them, they're always complaining and giving me grief here, it's quite normal my dear."

"Well, they shouldn't be talking so rudely, they have no manners. My dad wouldn't appreciate those comments, I know my dad helps this clinic by donating lots of money, and so what if I come here," Zaynab voiced.

"You're quite a mature child. Yes you're right. There's absolutely nothing wrong in coming to this clinic, you are welcomed at any time here. Now, how can I help you?"

"I had a leech stuck in between my toes. This kind old man came to my rescue and took the leech off. But my foot started bleeding and he suggested I see you to get it checked out," Zaynab explained.

"Very well, you've done the right thing, my dear. It's always a good idea to have it looked at. I can't see anything serious although your feet do need washing so I can see a little better," the doctor insisted.

Zaynab was taken to another room by the nurse and given some water and a container to wash her feet. By then, she had thick mud all over her feet and the doctor really couldn't see her toes properly. The crowd outside were moaning and complaining more than ever before. Not only did they believe that Zaynab shouldn't be there, they thought Zaynab had jumped the queue as well. They banged on the walls and doors, they shouted and taunted. They almost became restless and violent.

The doctor stepped out of his room and standing at the porch addressed the long impatient queue.

"If you lot don't stop moaning, I will close the clinic and you will not be seen today, I promise," he shouted. "Be patient and stay quiet. I don't want any remarks from anyone here. I am the doctor on call and I will see whomever I wish. Besides, you know my rule is to see children first then adults... so enough with the complaints or I shall send you home."

Zaynab could not believe her luck. The doctor exactly understood what she was saying before. He was on her side, and he'd already scolded the rude people in the queue. Zaynab felt much better. It was a kind of sweet revenge.

"Thank you doctor, thank you for seeing me and thank you for having a word with them out there."

"Not to worry my dear, all you need on your foot is a clean up with some antiseptic cream and I'll just put on a plaster for you," the doctor said. "I'm more than happy to see you. You have good manners. I never get a thank you from that lot out there. They just want to be seen, served and demand medicine whether they need it or not," he continued.

"Okay doctor, I'll tell my dad all about you and how kind you've been to me today," Zaynab said cheerfully.

"Yes, please pass on my salaams to him, I know your dad very well. By the way, you're better off taking this back exit to go home. You want to avoid being seen by those people out there, you know they'll start again when they see you," said the doctor, smiling.

"Yes, probably a good idea doctor," agreed Zaynab as she walked out with a big grin.

Chapter Thirteen

Budharail Primary School

After the agreement with Imam Sahib to teach Zaynab and her brother the Bangla language, it was decided to take their learning to the next level. Both Zaynab and her brother had learnt enough Bangla now and were ready to understand other subjects taught in Bangla. It was only a matter of time before Zaynab would have joined the village school and now that time had come. It was time to enrol in Budharail Primary School. Their learning with their dad was on track but he now wanted them to taste the student life in a village school.

"You'll enjoy the experience children, you'll see," Dad promised.

"We don't mind but it's gonna be so weird, going to school everyday," said both brother and sister.

"I shall talk to the head teacher to take you both into his class, he actually teaches your age group," confirmed Dad.

"What year will I go into then Dad?" Zaynab asked.

"Erm...that's quite a difficult one, I think you'll both be in the same class because you're only a year apart."

"You mean both of us will learn the same things in class?" Zaynab's brother asked.

"Yes, I don't think there's enough classrooms and teachers to accommodate each year by the age groups, so they have to teach some of the classes with mixed ages. It'll be up to the teacher to differentiate between the levels of ability," explained Dad.

"Well, what exactly are we going to learn there?" they enquired.

"You'll be doing Literacy, Numeracy, Science, and Bangla lessons. Those are the four subjects you'll need to focus on for now. Don't worry about the other subjects. The core subjects will do just fine," Dad insisted.

"Cool, we'll get to see who's good at what in the classroom, can't wait actually come to think of it," shrieked Zaynab's brother all excited and eager to go.

A few days later Zaynab and her brother got ready with their school bags and plodded behind their dad to go and enrol at the village primary school. They were nervous but at the same time excited about meeting the other children and their teacher.

"Welcome my children, welcome," greeted the head teacher. "Your father's been telling me all about you two. I'm so happy to see you both."

Zaynab's dad and the head teacher spoke privately for a few minutes and agreed that it would be most suitable for Zaynab and her brother to be taught by the head teacher as he spoke fluent English. The head was in charge of the final year group and even the children in his class spoke good English. It was ideal, thought

Zaynab's dad. After a few minutes with the head teacher, Zaynab's dad said his goodbyes and headed back to the house.

"Okay children, it's your first day in class so we'll take it nice and easy today," said the head teacher. The class was in the middle of a mathematics lesson and everyone had copied off the blackboard the examples of the acute angles that the teacher had drawn.

"Class, please write down the following..." he demanded in a very stern voice. "An acute angle is always less than ninety degrees," he shouted out, and everyone very quickly jotted down the words. "Today we'll be finished looking into acute angles and we'll be moving on to obtuse angles next. But since we still have a few more minutes left, I'd like you to finish off your maths lesson today by drawing me ten different acute angles with ten different measurements," he instructed.

Zaynab had a big smile on her face and so did her brother. They had just covered that topic at home with their dad. Not only had they done pages and pages of acute angles but they had already learnt the other angle types too. This is gonna be an easy ride, thought Zaynab and her brother. A few minutes later, the class stopped.

"It looks like we've reached the end of the mathematics lesson," said the head teacher glancing at the big wall clock. "Class, please pull your English books out now, thank you," he demanded.

The English lesson was gonna be interesting, thought Zaynab. "I wonder what they'll be doing for English," she muttered to herself.

"Class, what a good time for our newcomers to join us," declared the teacher. "We're having a reading week this week and all you have to do is listen to the novel that we're reading in class."

The head teacher went and opened his brief case and pulled out a copy of the novel.

"Mrs Frisby and the Rats of NIMH," he muttered. "That's the novel we're reading in class."

This was quite a tough story for the year five class and the teacher had to summarise and water down each passage after he read it. The teacher read a full chapter and the fantasy and science fiction grabbed the attention of the whole class. Zaynab had never before come across such descriptions of humanlike personalities in rats. The very animal that was considered a mere rodent in the village was given extraordinary abilities in the story. She was in the perfect setting to take full advantage of this story, she could imagine their every move and plot and thoroughly enjoyed the chapter of the novel. As the teacher read on, the class was gripped with the suspense and intrigue that the story presented.

"So how did you find that?" asked the teacher as he closed the book for another lesson.

"Sir, that was one of the best stories I've heard about rats. I can't wait to hear more of the story, Sir," Zaynab shouted in sheer excitement.

"Yes, I thought you might enjoy it. I know I couldn't put it down when I first read it twenty years ago."

"Wow! That must be a very old book," Zaynab mumbled. Suddenly the bell sounded and the class rushed to put their things back inside their desk trays. It was lunchtime and all the children headed back home for lunch, as there was no facility for school dinners in the village school. Only the teachers remained behind as they often travelled from far distances. They brought with them their Tiffins, which mainly contained rice with fish, vegetable curries or dhal.

Zaynab and her brother headed back home with their rucksacks on their backs. They blended in well with the other village children. Since the school was just a few minutes walk through the village, it was quite safe for them to walk back home, alone. After all, they had now stayed in Bangladesh for so many months that they knew each an every inch of the village.

After lunch, Zaynab and her brother returned to class. All the other children had also returned.

"We will be having our Bangla lesson now, so class! Please pull out your writing books," the teacher demanded. The whole school experience was now about to change for Zaynab and her brother. Bangla was the strongest subject for everyone in the class. But it was the weakest for Zaynab and her brother. How will I keep up? And what level are they on? Zaynab wondered. The head teacher was already briefed about the level of Bangla that Zaynab and her brother had reached up to. Unfortunately it wasn't quite enough for the year five class they had joined. It was more suitable for the Year Three level.

The teacher wrote on the blackboard with the squeaking chalk. Zaynab wasn't used to hearing the chalk squeak as she had only used the whiteboards in school back in England. The writing on the backboard looked very neat but that didn't help. Zaynab was quite baffled trying to work out what the teacher had written.

"These are comprehension questions, please answer them in as much detail as you can," instructed the teacher. The other kids began to get busy, writing away. They looked down and were not moving left or right. They acted like robots, whizzing through the task. Zaynab felt a little frustrated, she couldn't write as fast as the other children could, and worse was the fact that she couldn't understand what was on the board. However, Zaynab could rest and breathe a sigh of relief. The head teacher had already planned a different task for her and her brother.

He pulled out a sheet from his briefcase and kindly asked them to copy from that sheet.

"That's more like it, Bayyah," said Zaynab.

"Yeah, this is what we were doing with Imam Sahib back in the bungalow," they confirmed.

Finally, the school day came to an end. Zaynab and her brother had thoroughly enjoyed their first day in school. It felt like a very, very long day but it was worth it, they thought.

Budharail Primary school wasn't a bad school at all. It had just enough facilities to enable the village children to gain at least basic education to the end of primary level. The head teacher was passionate and introduced challenging books like the one they had read in the English lesson. He believed in pushing the children and empowering them with the right tools before they moved on to the high schools.

The school, however, needed lots of attention in many areas of the curriculum, and Zaynab realised, when she compared it with her school back in England, that it missed a lot of other subjects and had no provision for P.E lessons. It only had classes up to year five and after this final year they had to move onto year six in the high schools. The nearest high school was in Sayedpur and Zaynab could remember clearly seeing the school on the way back from the big wedding.

"Bayyah! So what do you think of this school then?" Zaynab asked as they walked home.

"I guess it's not too bad. It's a bit too small to look like a school though," said Bayyah. "There's very little to do outside the classroom, but I'm not complaining, I like it," he confirmed.

"Yeah me too, I was a bit shocked when the teacher pulled out Mrs Frisby..." Zaynab admitted.

"Yeah, that is one nice story, you know I'm actually looking forward to the next lesson," Bayyah said. "Even if I don't learn anything else, I'm quite happy to get to the end of that book."

"Me too. I'm gonna buy that book when we go back to England," Zaynab vowed.

Zaynab and her brother had now reached home. "How was your first day in school then, did you enjoy the whole day?" enquired Mum. She had forgotten to ask at lunchtime as she rushed around trying to get their food ready.

"Yeah Mum, don't worry. We like school all right! Put it this way Mum, we're not about to quit anytime soon," they said, giggling at the same time.

Chapter Fourteen

Fantasy Kingdom, Dhaka

It was almost coming to the end of Zaynab's gap year from school. Zaynab and her family had now enjoyed all the six exotic seasons. She watched the late autumn *Hemontho* turn to the misty, dry and chilly *Sheet* season. She saw how the dry and damp-free climate allowed the village children to bring out their tennis rackets and footballs and spend long days in the fields playing. She waved goodbye to the dry, dusty and chilly climate only to welcome the favourite of the climates, the *Boshonto* season. The spring was where the parties, *melas* and all types of outdoor activities happened.

The whole country even got involved in the local politics in this season and Zaynab enjoyed watching the different clusters of people chanting political slogans as they marched past the village fields.

Some represented *Nawka* the boat, others stood for *Chathi* the umbrella. These flashed in Zaynab's head as they marched with big posters and continuously repeated chants on the handheld speakers.

"Dhaner-shishe-boot-den," shouted a group of people in her area. It was the distinctive party name Zaynab remembered, it meant 'rice crop.' The people were chanting, "Vote for the rice crop party".

The fields were littered with posters, ribbons and advertisement cuttings from the election campaigns. Zaynab got overwhelmed and even she began to support one of the parties. Her dad had taken them to the stalls all over the field and she bought a key ring with a bright rice crop image on it.

"I support Dhaner Shish," she muttered to herself.

It was a nice sunny morning in February, and Zaynab sat on her house veranda recalling, one after the other events relating to each season. She had just seen the end of the politics spell and was wondering as to what the next thing in store was. She noted that the village life was filled with adventure and thrills. Zaynab could see through the decorative veranda grille panels, the beautiful betel nut trees and the exotic palm trees, jostling from side to side against the mild spring breeze. She saw how everyone went about doing their daily errands and how the other children like her were never bored because they always had something to do.

Zaynab had enjoyed some of the best months in her life in the village and could now understand her dad's comments about it when they had first arrived in Sylhet. The highlight of her stay in Bangladesh was no doubt the mighty trip to St. Martin's Island. She cherished those memories even if it had only been a few months ago. She recalled the first day when they travelled on the Emirates bus from Dhaka and her dad mentioning so many adventurous places in Dhaka that they would see if time permitted. She also recollected her mum's words about visiting those places once they had settled in the village. Suddenly an idea flashed in Zaynab's head. It was like a light bulb moment. Should they not be planning to go to those places now that everyone was settled in the village life?

Indeed, Zaynab considered herself as one of the villagers. She ran wildly in the muddy patches, she swam like a fish, she played in the cold, and she played in the heat. She went to school and she helped to cook. Zaynab was fully captivated by the village life that was for sure. She now got off from her seat and went back in the house.

"Mum?" she called.

"When are we going back to Dhaka, to see some of the great attractions?" Zaynab fired away. "I'm particularly interested in going to the Fantasy Kingdom, is that likely to happen?"

"You can ask your dad, when he comes home, dear, I'm sure something can be arranged."

A little while later when Zaynab's dad had arrived, she fired away the same question.

"Fantasy Kingdom! Of course we'll be going there. I was just about to plan the trip considering we're going back home soon," Dad surprisingly revealed.

"Hurray! Great news, when are we going then?" she asked again, jumping up and down.

"Okay, I'll arrange it for Saturday. We need to ask for a few days leave from your school, and then I don't see a problem."

Zaynab rushed to find her brother; she was ecstatic and really looking forward to another exciting trip. This time it would be by road and she would again see the lush green spectacular scenery and wonders, but this time in the season of *Boshonto*. The trip would be the last one before they headed back to England and she was going to make the most out of it.

"Bayyah! Dad's planning to take us to Fantasy Kingdom on Saturday!" Zaynab screeched in excitement.

"Really! I've heard so much about that place. It's like a mini Disneyland they say!" Bayyah said.

"Well whatever it's like, we're certainly about to find out soon," Zaynab confirmed.

Zaynab had now been living as a village resident for nearly a year. Despite her dad arranging for some spectacular and mighty trips in that time, they had kind of got dragged into the everyday school life and had been busy after school learning with the Imam Sahib. The status quo was beginning to have a toll on them and they couldn't have had a better time to go away again.

So, on Saturday morning the family awoke early and began to prepare for the exciting trip to Dhaka Fantasy Kingdom. A mini bus was hired so that a few more friends or relatives could tag along with them. As usual, Zaynab's brother requested Dulon join them as he made very good company. Zaynab learnt that travelling became more fun when she had more people with her.

By now she had made dozens of friends all over the village. One particular friend she was close to was Hafsa, a girl of the same age, who lived just a few houses away from Zaynab's.

After asking Hafsa's parents for permission to take her, she was overjoyed to have her own companion just like her brother did. After all, she was almost a year older than when she had arrived, and didn't fancy hanging around with the boys all the time.

The bus set off around nine o'clock in the morning and it was estimated that they would arrive at the Ashulia Highway for about one o'clock in the afternoon. Fantasy Kingdom was situated in the Ashulia village area and the driver boasted about the number of times he'd been there, dropping off families like Zaynab's.

"So we shouldn't get lost on the way then," remarked Zaynab's dad jokingly to the driver.

The atmosphere in the bus was buzzing, everyone was ready to go on another adventure trip. For some like Hafsa and Dulon it would be their first trip to any type of amusement park. They all waved goodbye to the rest of the village neighbours and in a flash drove off towards the west, heading via Sylhet.

After a nice scenic drive for about three and a half hours, the minibus reached the Dhaka-Mymensingh Highway.

"We're only about five miles away folks, looks like we're close," announced the driver.

Everyone in the bus suddenly began to get excited again, they put away their cups and packets of munchies and began to tidy themselves up.

"Dad! How long will we stay in Dhaka?" asked Zaynab.

"Erm...just a few days I think. We'll be staying at the Motel Atlantis Resort Hotel. And if we get a chance we can also visit Nandon Park which shouldn't be too far from here," confirmed Dad.

"You can also visit the Water Kingdom which is right besides the Fantasy Kingdom," suggested the driver.

"Yes, if you really enjoy it, we can always add a few more days on the trip," Dad said, smiling.

The bus finally stopped at the designated car park. Zaynab's family first checked into the hotel and organised the rooms for everyone and then headed back out to the famous Fantasy Kingdom Park.

"Wow, this is breathtaking, it dwarfs Alton Towers for sure!" exclaimed Zaynab's brother.

"Yeah it's more like Disneyland Paris, I'm chuffed we've come here," cried out Zaynab.

Hafsa and Dulon were gobsmacked, they hadn't even seen such things on television, and for them the impact was greater.

"I can't believe this, it's like we're in a dream," Dulon muttered.

"Well I think it's a dream come true for you and and for us too!" Zaynab expressed.

"Well what are we waiting for? Let's get stuck in, Dad!" Zaynab and her brother cried out and in they all went through the splendid gates of the park.

Fantasy Kingdom rose above everyone's expectations. It was elegant, beautiful and so professionally created. It looked like they were in fact somewhere in Disneyland. The whole park was buzzing and bustling with children and grown ups as you would expect in any theme park. There was a fifteen hundred feet long roller coaster, which dominated the site. Close by was also the Water Kingdom, which was connected by an aquarium tunnel, taking people from one to the other. There was just so much going on that Zaynab and her family didn't know where to start.

"Hey, can you see that massive flume ride like Alton Towers?" shouted Zaynab. "Can't wait to get on that."

"Amazing! Look at the dinosaurs, they look real,"

called out Zaynab's brother.

"Yes and look over there, there's a bumper cars area and a giant games arcade," Dad pointed out.

"There's a huge Go-Kart platform, we can go to that too." They both pointed out.

There was the Santa Maria Viking Ship, there was the Arabian flying carpet, there were fun and enjoyable water rides, there were horse racing rides. Plenty of stalls, souvenir shops and so much more. Zaynab couldn't wait, she jumped on the log flume ride and off she went.

"Hurray!" She shouted. "It's like I'm flying, oh, I love this so much," she yelled, screeched and giggled.

Zaynab's brother, Dulon and Hafsa joined in too.

"Well what are we watching for?" said Zaynab's dad, turning to Zaynab's mum and Luqman. "Let's all jump on and have fun!"

Zaynab screamed and shouted so much that she lost her voice. About an hour in to the park, everyone was exhausted. From the water rides they went to the roller coaster, from there they jumped on the Go-Karting track. It was great fun, exhilarating and therapeutic at the same time. For Dulon and Hafsa it was an experience they would be sharing with their families for a long time to come. The family moved through the glass aquarium tunnel.

"Bayyah! Look at the beautiful and colourful fish, they look fascinating," Zaynab said in utter amazement.

"Wow, they are nice, so colourful," uttered Bayyah.

"They're a fine collection of dazzling marine fish," commented Dad. "They just look amazing!"

The family now walked into the Water Kingdom. Everyone was prepared to do water activities and had worn the appropriate gear. They were going to finish off from the Water Kingdom for the day, and then return to their hotel rooms, as they would be soaking. There were giant water slides, a wave pool and all sorts of other activities for Zaynab and her family. The DJs blasted their traditional Bangla music and everyone looked like they had gone into a trance, dancing away and splashing about in the shallow waters.

"They dance so funny," Zaynab's brother commented.

"Well, they're just having fun, it's not a dancing competition you know," Zaynab replied to the snide comment.

Zaynab's family again wasted no time; they all huddled up together and jumped into the wave pool. It was crazy and fun, everyone ended up in different directions. It was safe for everyone to jump in and out; they had the floats, armbands and massive float rings that were found every few metres in the giant pool. They spent the next few hours simply playing water sports and rides until they could play no more.

"I think, we'll call it a day here now, we've always got tomorrow to come and bash the waters and go wild," Dad announced. Mum agreed. After all, they had been enjoying themselves non-stop since they had got there. Zaynab's family had a wonderful day at the Fantasy Kingdom, for a short time they had forgotten they were even in Bangladesh. It felt like they were somewhere in Europe or America.

This was probably because they had stayed in the village for so long that they had forgotten what it was like to be in a bustling and chaotic atmosphere with loud and blasting DJs playing their music.

Zaynab's family stayed for one more night at their hotel before they headed for Nandon Water Park, which wasn't too far off. Nandon Park was quite similar to the Water Kingdom with all the wave pool and water slides. The popular doom slide and the wave runner were packed with people. The water fun plaza area was like a wet playground and Zaynab's mum and her younger brother spent hours playing in there. The boat riding was so exhilarating and allowed for some calm and peace after the crazy screaming and shouting everyone had done. There was no doubt that the trip to Fantasy Kingdom and Nandon Park was the best way to sum up their year long trip to Bangladesh. It was the best few days in a long time, thought Zaynab and she jotted down and captured the dream-like moments in her diary. It was going to add more excitement to her collection of adventurous trips that she was so busy writing about. After the visit to Nandon Park, Zaynab's family finally headed back to Budharail all happy, invigorated and truly satisfied.

Chapter Fifteen

Good bye, Myna Bird

It was now April and the *Grishmo* sun beamed down fiercely. The mornings were hot and the afternoons were sweltering. It was almost a year since they first set foot on Bangladeshi soil in Dhaka. Next month, Zaynab's family would be returning back to England. It would be a magnificent year in their lives, which they could cherish, speak and write about for a long time to come.

Zaynab had thoroughly enjoyed her gap year from school. Well, the gap year from her school back in England that is. She had enjoyed the brief city life in Sylhet and the long village life in Budharail. She had seen the changes in the dramatic climate and witnessed the beauty of each season. She had tasted the exotic fruits and settled on favourites that she hadn't even known the names of. By now, she also spoke a good level of Bangla and knew all the cultural traditions. She had done everything a child could possibly do in the village: she played, she sang, she studied, she cooked, she cleaned, she swam, and she even stitched with thread and she read. She had seen rivers, canals, wetlands and seas. She had seen the lakes and all the earthquakes. Zaynab had done and seen an awful lot in the past year.

On the way back from school one day, Zaynab and her brother spoke of their wonderful past few months. They recollected those fascinating moments and were just expressing their sorrow of going back to England.

"Bayyah! Can you believe that we're going back next month?" Zaynab muttered.

"Isn't it sad, hey, I feel so connected to this life here, it's so outdoor and interesting, I couldn't say I was bored for even a day," Bayyah expressed.

"I know, Bayyah, we're not likely to have another year out of our lives with this amount of fun and adventure," she said regretfully.

"Well, we've got to count ourselves lucky enough I think, not many would be in our position, enjoying the things we've enjoyed," explained Bayyah.

"Yeah, I guess so Bayyah, but I'm gonna seriously miss this place," mumbled Zaynab. Just then, a voice from inside the house called both Zaynab and her brother. They both walked in and to their surprise they saw a beautiful bird in a cage.

"What's this Dad?" they asked curiously. "A bird?" they questioned with astonishment.

"Yes, it's actually a talking bird, a Hill Myna," answered Dad.

"Does it really talk, Dad?" they asked in sheer excitement.

"Yes, it's already trained to speak, it doesn't just mimic your words, it'll speak to you."

"Well how did this suddenly come about then?" asked Zaynab. This was a little difficult to take in. They weren't expecting anything like this at the end of a normal school day. They were just astounded at the discovery.

"One of your uncles came by when you were in school. He's leaving for his pilgrimage trip tomorrow and will be away for nearly a month," explained Dad. "He thought we could look after it till he comes back. He did mention to me, that it would be heaps of fun, so I took it in."

"Fantastic! Thank you so much Dad, for taking it in," cheered and praised both of them, jumping up and down in joy.

"Has it got a name, Dad?" Zaynab asked.

"Yes, it's called *Moyna,* you can say *Moyna* the Myna bird!" said Dad jokingly.

"Wow, nice and smart! What a name," Zaynab said.

"So, Dad let's get this right, we've actually got this bird for nearly a month?" Zaynab's brother quizzed.

"Yes, yes, for the last time, I'm telling you. You have a talking myna bird for a month," confirmed Dad.

"Now that's crazy! I can't believe this. I am just too happy to do anything now..." shrieked Bayyah.

"So what does it eat, Dad?" Zaynab enquired.

"It's a pretty much omnivorous bird. It'll eat fruit, nectar and insects I'm guessing," said Dad.

"Wow, that's easy. It'll be great fun catching insects to feed it," remarked Bayyah.

The next few weeks were so fun and exciting. Zaynab and her brother were simply hooked on spending time with the bird. They went out into the fields with Dulon and Hafsa. They were on a mission to catch insects. Grasshoppers were the myna bird's favourite. And there was no shortage of them in the giant pastures in the village area. They all took empty glass bottles each and separated in four different directions. They even played a game seeing how many grasshoppers each one could catch from each of the four cardinal directions. Would North win? Or would it be West? They had an hour to catch and return to the starting point. Zaynab was given South and like in all things she became competitive in this too. She was patient and determined to let South win and so she eagerly went in search with a hawk eye to catch as many grasshoppers as possible.

Zaynab ran through the fields, went in and out of the bushes, and investigated every plant and tree and every hill in the village to find grasshoppers. "Hey this is just cool, I've already caught half a bottle, and it's only been a few minutes," muttered Zaynab to herself. She continued in fascination.

The rest of them also disappeared in to the bushes. Zaynab's brother came across some with wings and some without. There were also small and large ones. He scooped every type and began to fill his bottle. But the master of this game was Dulon. He hadn't even moved much and he was almost finished filling his bottle. An hour later, all of them assembled at the starting point and began to compare each bottle.

"Looks like I won, I have the only bottle that's full to its top," said Dulon.

"I've not done bad you know, maybe one or two more would have filled mine up," said Hafsa.

"What's yours looking like Bayyah?" asked Zaynab.

"Yeah, I'm pretty good too. Mine is all full," said Bayyah.

Zaynab pulled out her bottle and she too had filled up right to the top. "So it looks like Bayyah and Dulon have tied," she declared.

"Not quite over yet," yelled Bayyah. He pulled open

127

the flap of his shirt pocket and indicated towards it. There were a few more grasshoppers in his shirt pocket.

"Ha ha!" he laughed. "With those in my pocket I think I can safely say that I'm the winner of today's grasshopper quest, yes North has won today," he rejoiced.

All of them excitedly went back to the house. Zaynab got a larger container with a lid and put some leaves and grass inside it. "Let's carefully put them all in here," she said.

"Yeah good idea, we can't possibly feed it all in one go now, can we?" posed Dulon with a sensible remark.

"You're right, we can feed it slowly and enjoy watching it feed on them," said Zaynab.

"Why don't we all take turns to feed it now," suggested Zaynab. She pulled out a thin toothpick and stuck a grasshopper at the end of it and pushed the grasshopper through the cage.

"Thank you, Thank you, Thank you," said the myna bird in a croaky voice. Everyone started looking at each other in utter surprise. They had forgotten that the bird could speak; they were totally oblivious to the fact that the bird in their house was a talking hill myna.

"Oh my god! Did you all hear that?" cried out Zaynab totally bewildered.

"Amazing! The bird just thanked you Zaynab, and so clearly too," said Bayyah.

Hafsa went next and fed it the same way.

"Thank you, Thank you, Thank you!" said the bird again.

"What's your name, bird?" asked Hafsa.

"My name is Moyna, I am Moyna, call me Moyna," said the bird jumping up and down.

"Its favourite number isn't three by any chance is it?" wondered Zaynab's brother. The bird seemed to repeat its answer three times every time it spoke.

"It's probably to emphasise the answer Bayyah, I mean Dad did say it's fully trained to speak," Zaynab explained.

"So, Moyna, can you understand us?" asked Bayyah.

"Yes, I can, I can," replied Moyna. "And no, three is not my favourite number," declared Moyna.

Zaynab's brother was dumbfounded; the bird had already picked up on his last comment.

"Chill out, Moyna, I was just joking, it just sounded a little weird to me that's all," explained Bayyah apologetically.

Moyna was a dark, jet-black feathered bird with a beautiful yellow and orange beak. It had patches of bright yellow skin and yellow wattles hanging off both side of its head. Its legs and feet were yellow and it looked like a strong but gentle bird.

"Okay, so are you hungry?" Zaynab asked.

"Yes, I am hungry, very hungry," replied Moyna.

And so they talked and fed Moyna until it was full. It was a new fascination in the house and Zaynab and her brother's outdoor activities dramatically decreased as they spent hours upon hours playing and talking to Moyna over the next few weeks. They went out each day to catch the grasshoppers, they talked about it in the school break times, they absolutely adored Moyna and they dreaded the day they would have to say goodbye to it.

It was now May and there was only a week left to go back to England. Zaynab's uncle had returned to Bangladesh after his pilgrimage trip was successfully completed. He arrived at Zaynab's house while they were in school.

"Oh I feel bad taking Moyna away, while they're still in school," said Zaynab's uncle.

"Why don't you wait till they're back, I mean, what's the rush?" insisted Dad.

"Yeah, I owe it to them, the poor kids will be gutted. They've done a marvellous job looking after Moyna though," he praised.

A few hours later Zaynab and her brother arrived back from school.

"*Assalamu alaikum* Uncle, how are you?" they greeted together.

"*Wa alaikumus salaam*, I am fine thank you, children. How was your day in school then?"

"Yeah, we gave in the letter that my dad wrote about leaving and going back, so it was quite sad. It's our last day in school tomorrow," they explained.

"Oh well, on that note of going back, I just want to say thank you so much for looking after Moyna so well. I heard all about the long days you spent hunting for Moyna and how you fed Moyna its favourite food every day."

"Yeah, we enjoyed it more than anything else. Uncle, we're gonna really miss Moyna you know."

"Yes, I believe that you will, it obviously can't be helped. Anyway, stay in touch when you get back and I'll tell you how Moyna's doing from time to time," insisted Uncle.

"Yeah, we definitely will, Uncle," they promised.

"Goodbye now Moyna," they said in one big voice and at that point Zaynab's uncle got up and covered the cage with a cloth. He waved goodbye to everyone and quite sharply made an exit. He might have done that purposely just in case Zaynab or her brother or even young Luqman burst into tears trying to hold it back.

"Goodbye, Goodbye, Goodbye!" came the voice in the distance and everyone in the family smiled and laughed with fulfilment.

Chapter Sixteen

Terminal one, Manchester

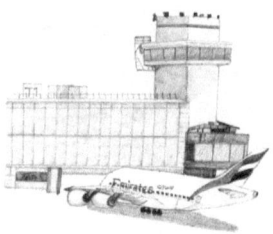

The day had finally come and Zaynab and her family had to leave Bangladesh. It was the end of a long gap year where the most extraordinary and unimaginable things had happened to Zaynab. She had come as a young child with no experience of rural life and was going back as a mature, experienced and a profoundly cultured girl. She was now like a compendium of knowledge, advancing in her Literacy, Numeracy and Science. She had also learnt the Bangla language well and could converse pretty fluently.

Zaynab had left no stone unturned in the village; she was immersed in a culture quite unlike anything found in England. It was going to be tough for her to leave such a life behind, a life so much orientated around the outdoor and water. A life that thrived on watching seasons change every two months. But Zaynab understood that she couldn't possibly live there for good, not unless she grew up and could make her own choice. She knew her real home was England and she had to study hard and get a good job there at some point in her life. She had to have her own money to live anywhere else. *Maybe I can just come to visit with my family each year,* she muttered to herself.

It was a very hot afternoon with blistering rays of the sun beating down on everything. The minibus had arrived and it was the same driver that had taken Zaynab and her family to Fantasy Kingdom. It was Zia, one of the best drivers in Sylhet.

"I've got the air-conditioning switched on full power," he shouted.

"Yes, most appropriate!" Dad shouted back.

The sweltering heat was so intense that the usual and classic comments of frying an egg on the bonnet were exchanged between the people gathered. The outside of the vehicle was just like a huge piece of metal taken out from a furnace.

"Careful! This one's got ceramics inside it," instructed Zaynab's mum.

"I think this is it, everything's loaded up Zia, you can lock the back doors now," instructed Dad.

One by one, each member of Zaynab's family got inside the vehicle. It was the worst moment in the whole year. It was a moment of reluctance and despair. Everyone had a melancholy expression and shared the heartache mutually. It appeared as though the entire village population had gathered to bid farewell to Zaynab's family. Almost everyone was tearful. How could they not be? They had known and lived with Zaynab and her family for the past year. They had become close neighbours and even closer friends. Standing amongst the crowd of people were Dulon and Hafsa, the two dearest friends of Zaynab and her brother.

"Goodbye, Bayyah and Goodbye, Zaynab," they both cried out. "We're gonna miss you so much," they mumbled almost bursting into tears. Zaynab opened the window and held Hafsa's hand for the last time. "I'm gonna stay in touch with you Hafsa, I'll write to you often," Zaynab promised.

Zaynab's brother did the same thing and promised Dulon he too would write to him.

They had to quickly close the windows due to the cool air escaping from the vehicle. They pulled back the hands and continued to wave from inside. Then suddenly, just before they set off, Zaynab's dad jumped out and went in the midst of the emotional crowd.

"What on earth is Dad doing?" yelled Zaynab.

"He's got a big sack in his hands, I wonder what he's up to?" said Bayyah.

"Don't worry children, he's only gonna dish out money to everyone there. His sack's full of five taka notes which he ordered yesterday," revealed Mum.

"Hurray! That's the best way to leave the village, leave a big smile on everyone's face, way to go Dad," cheered Zaynab and her brother. Zaynab's dad dished out money as a customary thing on the last day of leaving the village each time he visited. It was a nice sight to watch as everyone scrambled and competed with each other to grab hold of a five-taka note. Zaynab's dad also made sure that no one took more than one note, and he personally handed them to the children with his own hands.

"Thank you!" praised the children. "Thank you, very much," praised the grown ups.

"Thank you to all of you for coming to see us off," commented Zaynab's dad. He then jumped back in the vehicle and told Zia to start driving.

There was a sudden uproar in the crowd, everyone started waving and shouting goodbye. Zaynab and her family waved back and blew their kisses for the very last time.

The drive to Dhaka, Shahjalal International Airport was around the four hour mark. And since it was a nice and bright sunny day, there was no reason why they wouldn't arrive there on time. Generally, delays happened due to bad weather. The journey to the airport was filled with excitement too. For Zaynab, it was sort of the very first opportunity to sit back and submerge herself in the wonderful memories and good times in the village. It was also a time to just relax and enjoy the most pleasant, lush and scenic views that she would see in a long time to come.

A few hours later the vehicle arrived at the airport. The drive was extremely pleasant with no delays whatsoever. Zia the driver had done a fantastic job once again.

"Thank you, Zia, I'll certainly contact you, the next time we come," promised Dad.

"Yeah, Zia uncle. Thanks for being so good. You're the best driver around," praised Zaynab.

"It's a pity the airport name has changed from Zia to Shahjalal," joked Zaynab's brother cheekily.

"Ha ha, nice one lad!" Zia replied chuckling.

Zia gave them a hand, pulling out the luggage and helped Zaynab's dad all the way to the airport counter.

They all finally waved goodbye to Zia and Zaynab's dad gave him a final hug before he walked out and leaped back into his vehicle.

"That's it then, we're heading back to England," reminded Dad.

"Yes, we can't wait actually. There's a home sweet home waiting for us," the children voiced.

The call for Zaynab's flight was announced and fairly soon, her family boarded the giant aeroplane bound for Dubai International Airport. It was going to follow the same flight route as it did on arrival. They would have a stopover at Dubai for a couple of hours and then board the aeroplane, but this time bound for Manchester. A few hours later, the aeroplane touched down in Dubai. It was now the last leg of the flight. With no delays announced, Zaynab's family were able to board the aeroplane for one last time for their flight to England.

The flight to Manchester International Airport was about seven and a half hours long. It was no doubt a long-haul flight and Zaynab decided to divide her time well on the aeroplane. She played on the games for a few hours, watched a movie and even slept for another couple of hours.

Time passed fairly quickly and before anyone could guess, the pilot was on the microphone announcing his descent towards the airport. Moments later, the giant aeroplane touched down smoothly at Terminal One in Manchester International Airport.

"Wow, that was a smooth landing, *Alhamdulillah!*" uttered Zaynab's dad.

"Yes, all praise due to Allah, we've arrived safely back home," said Zaynab's Mum.

Zaynab's family waited patiently to get off the plane. They were completely shattered and spent. It had been a very long and exhaustive day starting from the village in Budharail and finally arriving in Manchester, England. Zaynab's uncles, aunties and other family members were waiting outside the arrivals area. Moments later, Zaynab's family walked through the arrivals gate and greeted all their eagerly awaiting family.

"Welcome back!" they shouted cheerily as they ran to embrace each other. "Welcome back to England."

THE END

www.ingramcontent.com/pod-product-compliance
Lightning Source LLC
Chambersburg PA
CBHW030131260626
47156CB00008B/2901